THE DARK SIDE

First edition. January 26, 2019.

Copyright © 2019 Jan Springer.

ISBN: 978-1386355441

Written by Jan Springer.

Also by Jan Springer

Club Rendezvous
Shy Girl

Cowboys Online : Moose Ranch
Cowboys for Christmas
Cowboys In Her Pocket
Loving Her Cowboys
Cowboys in Her Heart
Always Her Cowboys

Intimate Secrets
Intimate Lover
Intimate Kisses

Kidnap Fantasies
Jade's Fantasy
Zero To Sexy
Christmas Lovers

Pleasure Bound

A Hero's Welcome

A Hero Escapes

A Hero Betrayed

A Hero's Kiss

A Hero Wanted

Captive Heroes

Pleasure Bound Boxed Set

Pleasure Bound : COMPLETE SERIES SciFi Erotic Romance Boxed
Set

Tentacles Shifter Erotic Romance

Taken by Him

The Key Club

A Merry Menage Christmas

Sophie's Menage

Jewel's Menage

Jaxie's Menage

The Outlaw Lovers

Jude Outlaw

The Claiming

Colter's Revenge
Tyler's Woman
Resistance
The Outlaw Lovers
Alpha Outlaws Boxed Set

Vampira
Sweet Heat
Dark Heat
Wet Heat
Crimson Heat

Standalone
A Touch of Menage Boxed Set
Shades of Menage Boxed Set
Nice Girl Naughty
Sinderella Sexy
The Biker and The Bride
The Fire Within
Bared to Him
Pleasure Bound : A Futuristic Adult Romance Boxed Set
Merry Menage Kisses Boxed Set
Inner Girl Rising
Stripped Naked
Risqué Girl Delights Boxed Set
A Holiday Menage
Ménage À Trois
A Hitman for Hannah
Billionaire Boyfriend
Edible Delights

Vampira
Toygasm
The Dark Side

Watch for more at www.janspringer.com.

Everyone thought it was just the flu...but everyone was wrong.
With the help of two sexy men and a stray black cat, saber-yielding Jenna McKenna fights flesh-eating walkers during a desperate search for family members she hopes are still alive in the newly formed zombie apocalypse.

Good friends Tucker Brant and Ash Fleming have lost all their loved ones to the zombie-virus. The two men have tried to harden their emotions toward the saber-carrying woman who is intent on finding her family, but her strength and courage nurture a sizzling attraction the two men can't ignore. If they can live through the trek to the border and beyond, there just might be a future with Jenna. Until then, they'll enjoy her company as she warms their beds...

1

Chapter One

"Oh, come now, don't worry about the girls. It's just the flu. It's going around," Rick grumbled as he watched Jenna tuck his four-year-old twin daughters beneath the blankets of the Queen-sized bed the two girls shared. Irritation snapped through Jenna at his cavalier attitude.

Sometimes he just took things way too easily. That trait was one she really didn't like about him, especially now during what she perceived to be a possible health emergency for the girls.

His daughters looked awful. They were pale as ghosts and their foreheads very hot and sweaty. Their long blonde hair, normally shiny and bouncy, was stringy and oily and they'd only come down with the flu a couple of hours ago and mere minutes apart.

Boy, the medical warnings on tv weren't kidding when they said this flu was hitting hard and fast, despite the flu season being declared over last month. Now it was May and another strain of flu had hit with a vengeance.

"Seriously, we should take them to the emergency, Rick," Jenna said. But the two girls shook their heads.

"We don't wanna go to the hospital," Addison complained.

"We don't like doctors. They killed mommy," Madison said.

Oh great, what kind of crap was Rick feeding these kids? The girls' mother had died from ovarian cancer less than a year ago. The cancer had been detected too late for anything to be done, but Rick continued to blame the family doctor for ignoring his wife's concerns that she'd felt something was very wrong.

"Daddy, we want to stay here, in bed. We'll get better soon," Addison said and then she began to sob.

"Better really soon, daddy. You'll see," Madison added and then she too began to cry.

"Hey, see what you did, Jenna? You've upset them," Rick snapped with an anger she'd been seeing quite a bit lately. He yanked his blanket closer around his shoulders and frowned. He'd come down with the flu early this morning. He'd been complaining of a severe headache, chills, and nausea.

Thankfully the company she worked for as a software engineer had emailed yesterday stating they were closing down until further notice to the flu pandemic, so she'd be able to stay home to look after him and the girls.

"You kids stay right here in bed and rest. The MacMillan's are tough. We don't need any doctors. We can beat this flu. Right girls? We're not wimps, like Jenna," Rick said and then he stifled a cough.

Oh great. Make me out to be the bad guy.

Twin blonde heads nodded at him and then when the girls turned to look at Jenna, they scowled at her. Their frowns shot a volley of icy chills through her. Gosh, they suddenly looked *evil*. She resisted the impulse to pack her bags and leave the apartment right then and there.

Man, what was wrong with her? They were just two innocent kids. Why would she unexpectedly be so afraid of them? She must be tired. It had been a long day and it was time for all of them to get some sleep.

She clapped her hands together and feigned excitement.

"Okay, how about I sing to you until you fall asleep," Jenna said. She pulled up a chair beside their bed and sat down. The girls liked it when she sang, even if Rick didn't.

"I'm going back to bed and try to sleep this crappy shit off. See you all in the morning," Rick grumbled and thankfully he left the room without another word.

"Daddy's mad at you, Jenna," Addison said with a pout.

"He's always mad at you, lately," Madison added with a shake of her head.

"That's okay. He hasn't been feeling well. Once the flu is gone, everyone will be in a better mood," Jenna assured.

Madison was right. Rick was pissed off at her more than he was nice. Maybe it had been too soon for her to give up her place in order to move into this apartment with them. But she'd thought there had been something worth exploring between them and she had hit it off very quickly with the twins. The first couple of months had been great, but yeah lately, something was off.

Maybe he'd found another woman or figured out they just weren't that compatible. Maybe she'd leave him before he dropped the breakup bomb on her. But she'd grown so fond of the girls that she wasn't sure she could make a disconnect. A swell of emotion clutched at her throat and she quickly swallowed it down. Now was not the time to abandon everyone. She'd see them through this sickness and hope she didn't come down with it too.

Jenna frowned as she watched the girls shiver beneath their blankets. Their teeth chattered together like little bones hitting each other. She didn't like their red-rimmed glassy-eyed looks. Didn't like that she was giving in to them so easily too, but Rick was their parent and she couldn't go against his wishes. Besides, she'd seen on last night's news that the emergency departments were overwhelmed. It might be best to keep the girls here and have them rest. Thankfully they weren't puking or anything like that. At least not yet.

Jenna began to sing their favorite song, and before long their eyelids drooped. That would be the fever-reducing meds kicking in. She'd given them some half an hour ago when they'd complained of body aches and of being cold.

Finally, the girls fell asleep and Jenna sighed in relief. She truly sucked at medical emergencies and panicked when anyone got sick.

Maybe she *had* overreacted? Maybe Rick was right, and the girls just needed rest and they would beat this late spring flu.

Quietly she left their bedroom, leaving the door open in case one of them cried out. Down the hall, she peeked in on Rick. He was fast asleep, lying on his back, with an arm draped over his forehead. She grimaced at his white complexion. Gosh, he looked like death warmed over. She'd stay on the couch tonight.

Jenna didn't know how long she'd slept, but a strange brush-brush noise snapped her from her deep sleep. Her heart hammered against her chest and she struggled to open her eyes and orient herself as to her whereabouts. Slowly she remembered she'd fallen asleep on the couch and that Rick and the kids had come down with the flu.

Thankfully she still didn't feel sick and when she sat upright she tried to figure out what kind of strange sound drifted through the dark apartment. It seemed cool in here too and it smelled gross. She gazed out the nearby apartment window and noticed the nighttime security lights in the office building directly across the street were dark.

A freaking power failure? Seriously?

Shit. A power failure was not what they needed right now with everyone sick. Jenna muttered a soft curse, pushed away the blankets, slipped on her robe, and walked over to the window to get a better look. Uneasiness whipped through her when she spied darkness everywhere. Towering buildings were black and there were hardly any cars on the road below.

This was weird. New York City never slept. There were always people and cars on the street.

Man, she hadn't seen a widespread power outage like this since the summer of 2003.

Cyber-terrorist attack to the electrical grid came to mind.

Quietly she reached for the flashlight that Rick kept on a shelf near the tv. She switched on the light and located the emergency radio on the same shelf. She flicked on the radio and kept the volume low.

"Everyone is dying from the flu," said a reporter in a shaky voice.
What the fuck?

Jenna shook her head and choked back a laugh. This had to be someone joking about the flu epidemic. The man continued to speak in a low voice as if he didn't want someone to hear him.

"They die and then they come back. They look like they might be alive. But they aren't. They look dead. They smell awful. I don't know how long I have left to live myself because I got the flu. But I have to get the news out. Stay away from the dead ones. Once they turn, their dark side emerges. They get violent. They're..." the broadcaster hesitated and then he continued.

"They're killers. They won't know you. They are starving and they will eat you. Run for your lives. Run!"

Oh, what a bunch of crap! What kind of sick puppy makes fun of the flu?

That brushing sound that had awoken her rattled through the living room again. She'd check the other stations later. First, she needed to check out that creepy sound and that awful smell.

Jenna switched off the radio and shone the flashlight onto the battery-operated wall clock. It read four thirty a.m..

Good, it would be light soon. In the meantime, she needed to locate that noise before it woke up Rick and the girls. She angled the yellow beam of light into the hallway. The girls' bedroom was the first one and that's where the sounds came from. Maybe the girls were up already? Feeling better?

Oh, that would be so cool.

But as she strolled along the hall, the rancid smell overwhelmed her senses and Jenna quickly covered her nose and breathed through her mouth. The stench was coming from the girls' room. The girls and their dad shared the one bathroom so maybe the toilet had overflowed after one of them had used it?

First, she'd check on the girls and then she would take care of the bathroom. As she swung the beam of light into the dark room, she expected to find the twins sitting on their bed playing with their Barbie dolls. But the instant she dreamed up that scenario she realized they wouldn't be playing because it was dark. The flashlight beam splashed onto the bed and at first Jenna couldn't register what she was seeing, so she just stared.

Rick was in there. He was leaning over one of the girls. It was Addison. Had she gotten worse? But then Jenna noticed the blood. Crimson red soaked all the blankets and Addison was drenched in blood.

Madison was crawling in jerky movements from beneath the blankets toward her sister. Her eyes were vacant and red-rimmed. Her mouth was open and her teeth were clacking together.

Jenna watched in stunned horror as Madison lifted Addison's limp pale arm and took a bite out of her. A squishy sound ripped through the air and streams of blood spurt everywhere as Madison's teeth ripped off a piece of Addison's flesh.

What the hell? Am I having a nightmare? I need to wake myself up! This is horrible!

Jenna tried to scream as a rush of fear gripped her, but only a small pitiful squeak came out of her mouth.

The sound grabbed Rick's attention and he slowly turned his head toward her. She stopped breathing when she saw his gray face.

His eyes looked dead. Lifeless. His nose twitched as he sniffed the air. Blood dribbled down his chin and he was chewing on something. His nose and teeth were covered in blood and Jenna's gaze dropped to what Rick held in his hand.

An arm? Addison's arm? Had Rick died from that flu? Had he turned into one of those living dead? Was he feeding on his daughter?

She wanted to scream again. Instead, she began to shake as revulsion grabbed hold. Maybe this was reality?

"Rick?" she squeaked.

This is not happening. Wake up. Wake up!

Why wasn't she waking up?

Sickness crawled through her and Jenna stumbled backward. As she did, the flashlight beam splashed over Addison's lifeless, bloodied body. The little girl's eyes were unseeing as she stared into oblivion.

Oh, my God. Addison was dead, and her father and sister were eating her?

Suddenly Rick was shuffling toward her and Jenna knew she needed to run. Knew that life would never be the same again...

"Hey, wake up. Come on, let's wake up, babe." A rough shake of her shoulder and Ash's voice tore through Jenna like a bullet. She came awake with a start, grabbing her saber and even before she knew what she was doing, the tip of the blade was already pressing against Ash's jugular.

There was no fear in his eyes. No surprise. Only amusement.

"Shit, Ash, you've trained her well," came Tucker's chuckle.

The sound of a gun cocking made Jenna hesitate on sliding that blade tip right into her mentor's neck and watching red blood gush freely. For a split second, she wanted to see bright red blood, full of life, instead of the rotten grey liquid that oozed out of the zombies that she killed.

Her hand shook ever so slightly, giving away her true feelings of barely held self-control.

Ash's Adam's apple bobbed and the gesture snapped Jenna back to reality. Although Ash irritated the crap out of her, she didn't want him dead.

"Easy, babe," Ash said in a cool voice and gently pushed aside the blade.

Behind Ash, Tucker stood with a gun pointed at her head.

Son of a bitch.

Chapter Two

Tucker *would* pull the trigger, despite the fact he was screwing her brains out every chance he got. Ash and Tucker were best friends and they had made it clear to her that until they deemed her a worthy zombie slayer, she would be killed if she attempted to kill one of them. And sometimes, she really was tempted to do that. In this new world, she had no patience for men and their demands.

"You should know better than to wake me up when I'm in a dream. I could have killed you," Jenna spat. Fury stormed through her and it was hard to control her rage immediately following the nightmares that continued to ravage her. She barely heard Tucker uncock his gun.

They were all on edge. Sleeping out in the open did that, despite taking turns at sentry duty.

It had been well over four months since she'd escaped Rick and Madison and the hoards of zombies that had quickly taken over because of the deadly flu. She'd been trying for that long just to get out of the state and head back home to Ontario, Canada where her family lived. That is if they were still alive. She stifled the thick flow of emotions that threatened to make her cry.

She'd been stupid. She should *never* have left her parents and her siblings. But she'd accepted a job as a computer software engineer at a firm here. The money had been too good to turn down but getting dumped into a zombie apocalypse far from home without the support of family, really sucked.

"Come on, get dressed, breakfast is ready. We need to eat fast and explore the farmhouse and look for some more supplies. I'll be back in a few minutes," Tucker said.

He slung his quiver of arrows over his bare shoulder, grabbed a fresh shirt and his crossbow out of the back of the truck and without explaining where he was going, he walked off toward the edge of the meadow where she'd seen a creek yesterday.

Jenna returned her attention to the small smokeless fire nearby and grimaced at the breakfast of leftover rabbit laid out on a grill. Tucker had snared two white and very fat rabbits yesterday. Ash had skinned them and cooked them over the fire and the guys had had fresh meat along with a can of peaches last night. She'd settled on eating only the peaches, feeling so bad for the two rabbits.

She averted her gaze and looked at the two-story white planked, green trimmed farmhouse that loomed it the distance. It had appeared cozy enough to settle into for the night until a couple of zombies had tumbled out at them when Jenna had opened the front door. She'd quickly sliced off their rotting heads and stabbed their brains to put them out of commission. But the welcoming committee had turned her right off. After the guys had dragged the corpses into a nearby field, she'd insisted they sleep in the truck camper. But it had been too hot inside and so they'd settled a quarter mile away from the house in a meadow.

After supper, she and Tucker had strolled along a dirt road and then engaged in some hot and heavy sex up against a tree. When they'd returned to camp, they'd quickly fallen asleep, tangled around each other in a warm double sleeping bag while Ash had taken first watch for zombies. She'd taken the second round of sentry duty and unfortunately, that and her nightmares had screwed with her sleep cycle, not allowing her enough uninterrupted sleep, therefore, making her grumpy.

As she grabbed for her blouse, the sleeping bag slipped beneath her breasts, giving Ash a birds eye view of her nakedness. He was hunched over the fire, right across from her, stabbing a fork into a piece of rabbit. Tucker was nowhere in sight, so she didn't bother to cover her breasts.

She enjoyed the clench of her pussy as Ash's gaze grew dark with interest.

Both men were good looking. Tucker, clean shaven with short dark hair and Ash a bit rough looking with shoulder length, straggly hair and a dark beard and mustache.

She still hadn't had sex with Ash. She was attracted to both men, but only Tucker had made a move on her and she'd submitted to him, eager to feel the strength of a man penetrating her while she drowned in the pleasure of a quick climax. She had to admit, sex did ease her anger at the apocalypse, if only for a few hours. Maybe, she should suggest to Tucker that she get together with Ash too...

"How long do you think before we get to the border?" she asked as she continued to stare at him.

He shifted uneasily and she smiled inwardly. It was nice to see him get flustered.

"Tonight, unless we get killed in the meantime," he grumbled.

His gaze still hadn't strayed from her breasts and it encouraged her to allow the sleeping bag to dip even lower giving him a glimpse of her pussy. His gaze dropped to between her open thighs. Appreciation sparkled in his eyes.

She hadn't worn pajamas since a day after running from Rick's apartment. Mainly because she'd been stuck in the nightie while she'd wandered the streets, avoiding the sick and trying to find a couple of friends in nearby apartments. No one had answered when she'd buzzed them and finally she'd wrestled up the nerve to hop through an already broken window in a downtown department store where she'd been able to grab much-needed clothing, some weapons including the saber, a knife, along with a knapsack, tons of matches and some cooking utensils.

After that, she'd slept in her clothing and then nude after hooking up with the two men.

"So how long are you going to keep staring at me?" Ash suddenly asked.

"Until you decide you no longer want to stare at me," she retorted.

"Suit yourself," he whispered. He shook his head and frowned.

They stared at each other for the longest time and then finally, he ripped his gaze from her nakedness and focused his attention back to the strips of rabbit that sizzled on the grill. She'd never been forced to eat wild game before, but she had to admit the fresh meat did smell good.

Ash turned the meat again and her mouth watered at the scent of it.

"You'd best cover yourself," Ash suddenly warned in a thick voice.

"Why? Don't you like what you see?" Jenna teased. She loved the flare of heat in his dark green eyes. She wasn't stupid. She knew when someone was interested.

"You belong to Tucker. I don't fuck his women."

"Maybe you should start. You don't know what you're missing," Jenna said softly.

Gosh, but she sure was being bold this morning. She'd never been this way before the Zombie Apocalypse. She'd been a prude in bed and out, having slept with only one man one time before hooking up with Rick and he'd been a boring missionary position man.

But the Apocalypse had changed her. Made her realize any hour could be her last on Earth due to the rotters who now way outnumbered the survivors. And every day there were less and less live people as one by one they committed suicide, got sick and then undead because of the flu, or got eaten.

"Maybe you should get dressed," Ash suddenly said. There was something in his voice that instantly made Jenna alert. She smelled it before she even saw it. A deadhead was close.

Too close!

Instinctively she grabbed her saber. Sensing the walker was almost upon her, she swung her weapon in a wide arc right behind her. At the same time, she was rolling out of her sleeping bag and in a flash jumped to her feet just in time to see a female teenage zombie in tattered clothing fall right onto where Jenna had been sitting mere seconds earlier.

The rotter was missing a leg. Jenna located the leg she'd just chopped off. It lay in the grass nearby.

Rage bit through her.

"You son of a bitch!" she yelled at Ash.

He didn't appear in the least bit fazed at her narrow escape as he continued to sit on his haunches leisurely turning the pieces of rabbit. She had no doubt he would have let her get bit. Would have let her die.

"Number one rule, sweetheart. Never get so distracted that you don't know what's going on around you. Have I not taught you any better?" he said coolly.

Seriously? He had the nerve to show that he was disappointed in her?

Anger burst through her. She grabbed her blouse, thrust it on and quickly did up the buttons.

Man, this zombie survival shit was too freaking stressful. She should just abandon the two men and travel the rest of the way to Canada alone. If she couldn't even rely on them to watch her back, then what good were they?

Jenna struggled against the urge to cut off Ash's head. Instead, the clacking of teeth caught her attention. Deadhead was hungry. Time to put her out of her misery.

Jenna drove the tip of the saber into the rotter's left eye and grimaced at the sucking sound as the blade sliced through the skull and into the brain. The walker stopped moving, its grotesque mouth paralyzed into the open position.

Revulsion shivered through Jenna at the cold slimy flesh that gave way beneath her hands as she picked up the heavy leg and tossed it onto the torso. Then she grabbed the walker by its shoulders. Her stomach rolled with nausea at the waves of stench rolling off the corpse and she quickly pulled the body off her sleeping bag and dragged it into the meadow about twenty or so feet.

When she returned to camp, she could still smell the decaying person, but there was no use in complaining. The men would only tell her to drag it out farther if she didn't like it.

"Looks like you had a little bit of trouble while I was gone," Tucker said as he strolled into camp.

Irritation soared at the sound of his easy-going voice but her annoyance quickly vanished as she laid eyes on him. She had to admit, he did look sexy dangerous. He wore jeans and a dark blue tee shirt with short sleeves that showcased his bulging biceps. She noted he'd taken the time to shave and his dark brown hair was damp. He'd done a quick wash in that nearby creek.

"Your asshole friend decided not to warn me of an incoming walker," Jenna snapped.

"Your woman was too busy showing me her breasts and her pussy to notice she was in danger," Ash replied calmly.

Shock whipped through Jenna. He'd ratted her out!

She expected Tucker to get angry at her for being so wanton, but he shrugged his shoulders, crouched down beside Ash, and began forking some rabbit onto a tin plate.

"No worries, babe" Tucker said as he looked at her. There didn't appear to be any anger on his face or in his voice. He almost seemed...pleased?

"I've already seen that you can be a handful. Must have something to do with that fiery red hair. One of these days, the both of us will cool that anger burning inside of you. In the meantime, I'm starving. Let's eat. Then we need to do some exploring," Tucker said.

To her irritation, Ash smiled and winked at her. She resisted the urge to curse him out.

What the heck did Tucker mean by both of them cooling her anger? She wanted to ask that question but thought better of it. He probably meant chopping off her head. Odds were, she wouldn't be around much longer to find out what he meant anyway. Not after what had just happened with Ash not warning her of danger. They were unreliable.

Besides, why should she care what Tucker thought about her flirtations with Ash? Tucker didn't own her. She was a free agent in this new world. She would sleep with whomever she pleased.

Both men got quiet and to her surprise, Ash offered her a tin plate containing a choice part of the rabbit along with two halves of tinned peaches.

Despite her anger, she accepted the offering. She was hungry and she managed to gobble down the food in record time. Despite eating quickly, the guys ate faster and by the time she finished they were already heading toward that farmhouse. It was finder's keepers with these guys. Whatever they found, they kept. Whatever she found, she kept. Jenna grabbed her saber and hurried to catch up with them.

Ash grinned as he scooped up the box of condoms from inside the night table drawer in the second-floor bedroom of the farmhouse.

These should come in handy one of these days.

He thrust the box into his knapsack.

When it came time for him to give Jenna what she needed, he would be prepared. Earlier, he'd lied when he told her that he didn't bed Tucker's women. Truth was, he and Tucker had shared several ladies in their past. That exquisite habit had stopped with the Zombie Apocalypse because since then they'd been too busy surviving to pay attention to their sexual cravings.

But having Jenna around brought their needs screaming to the forefront. Tucker had given into his desires rather quickly where she was concerned, but Ash had stifled his urges, not wanting to become physically or emotionally involved with Jenna.

The woman didn't like him and she was a *big* distraction. If her nightmares and the way she awoke ready to kill, were an indication, she carried baggage. Hell, they all did.

But if she survived long enough, and proved she was a worthy warrior, then maybe he would tame her fury with some hot and heavy sex. In the meantime, he'd keep his pecker in his pants and focus on surviving.

Late yesterday they'd encountered two zombies who'd been trapped inside the farmhouse and their sickly undead stench still permeated the air despite the corpses having been removed. The man and woman had both been shot through the heart. Perhaps they hadn't known that they would rise from death after killing themselves. The only way to not return after dying was a shot or knife to the brain.

Something written on the mirror in bright red lipstick urged Ash to take a closer look.

The words SAVE BABY had been scrawled on the mirror. Ash grimaced. Was there a kid around here? Why would they shoot themselves and leave a baby here alive?

Man, what had these people been thinking? Perhaps the flu had made them delirious?

He moved away from the mirror and as he neared a closed door at the far end of the room he withdrew his knife from his thigh holster. He really should get out of here and warn the others that there could be more zombies around up here. But even as he thought it, he knew Tucker and Jenna would remain alert. They had to be in order to survive. Jenna had learned that lesson earlier out in the meadow.

He'd spied the approaching zombie and he'd seen Tucker watching it too. He'd already had an arrow fixed in his crossbow, ready to fire and kill it.

But Tucker hadn't fired. Perhaps he'd been thinking the same thing as Ash. Test Jenna with this opportunity.

She'd reacted very quickly. He'd been impressed with her lightning speed at taking out the rotter.

He chuckled to himself. She was good with that saber. Maybe she'd survive this zombie apocalypse. Maybe he should change his mind and get his pecker out of his pants and have sex with her. Maybe...

He calmed his breathing and listened. He thought he heard something. A clattering of teeth? He wasn't sure if it came from the other side of the door or if it was just the wind making a tree branch or something else tap against the farmhouse.

Ash settled his hand on the doorknob and quietly turned. The door creaked ominously as he slowly pushed inward. He peeked inside and sighed in relief.

It was just a bathroom. No one here.

He holstered the knife, quickly stepped into the room and opened the medicine cabinet. He let out a soft chuckle.

Jackpot. Drugs. Pain medications. Ointments for itchiness and bug bites. First aid kit with bandages and alcohol. A thermometer.

Although they already had most of these items from previous raids on houses and pharmacies, it was always good to have a bit more because it was increasingly difficult to get medical and food supplies. They were staying away from the cities and towns due to the overwhelming population of walkers and the small amounts of violent people. That's why they'd taken to the country backroads with the camper truck as they made their way toward Canada.

He hoped their decision to head north before winter came was a good one. The idea was to find Jenna's family, head up to cottage country and pray for plenty of snow that would hopefully slow down the deadheads. He was already planning on laughing his ass off as he flew past the rotters on a snowmobile.

After raiding the medicine cabinet, he grabbed a roll of toilet paper and shoved it into his backpack too. Then he noted another closed door. Heard a clack-clack sound.

He lifted his knife from his holster again.

Shit. Here we go again.

Tucker kept his gun aimed in the direction of the flashlight beam as he descended the creaky wood stairs into the cold basement. An occasional cobweb licked his cheek or tickled his nose and the chilly air embraced him making him want to rush back upstairs, grab Jenna and just start making love to her. He needed warming up and remembering her soft moans as he'd sunk his shaft into her last night while he'd made love to her up against a tree, made him hot. He shouldn't be down here. He should be upstairs, relaxed and enjoying her company.

However, this was a farmhouse on a side road that had been missed by looters and he suspected the owners might have some canned or preserved food stored somewhere. He tensed as something scurried around down there. Probably a rat, but survival instincts made him overly cautious and he wouldn't assume anything unless he saw it.

Somewhere above him, the floorboards creaked. He'd left Jenna on the main floor, and he hoped it was her making the creaks and not another freaking deadhead, despite the trio making sure the first floor was clear upon entering minutes ago.

Man, he wished he could just find a nice secure place and settle down with her. All this tension of being constantly on guard was going to send him into an early grave from a heart attack.

His heart cracked against his chest like a battering ram as he stepped onto the stone basement floor. He stopped, stood still and then he slowly swung the flashlight beam.

The basement was open concept down here. Bare rock walls with spider webs dangled from the ceiling. There were a couple of mountain bikes, some old furniture stored in a corner and...

Tucker smiled as he spied a bunch of wood shelves lining one of the walls.

Jackpot.

He stifled a whoop of joy as he strolled over and gazed at the Mason jars filled with pickles, beets, beans and other goods. There were berry jams and jellies and baskets filled with carrots, yams, potatoes and other root vegetables. There was even a basket of bright red apples.

Man, it was going to be a bitch lugging all this shit up to the truck, but in the meantime, his mouth was watering as he reached for an apple. His eyes were going to orgasm with all this beautiful, colorful food.

He took a bite out of the fruit and sweet flavor sprayed over his taste buds making him moan.

Wow, this tastes so good!

A split second later fear snapped through him as he sensed a presence. Before he could react, something came down on his shoulder. The impact wasn't hard, but it was unexpected and the shock of it knocked him right off his feet. He landed hard on his ass and his flashlight flew out of his hand. It clattered onto the floor and rolled beneath one of the shelves leaving Tucker in complete darkness.

Shit! He couldn't see anything.

Not. A. Damn. Thing.

But there was something here. It had jumped on him. Tucker's stomach plummeted at his next thought. Maybe it had even bitten him. If it had he couldn't feel any pain. Nor did he have the time to investigate.

It was nearby. He could sense it. Could hear it and he needed to kill it before it killed him.

Oh man, this smells really bad.

Ash stood just inside the doorway and gazed into the bedroom adjoining the bathroom he'd just been exploring. This room was gayly decorated in blues and yellows. The walls were white, the furniture blue. The playpen was set in the far corner...and it was occupied.

The odor of decaying flesh had Ash wanting to shut the door again, but he also knew what he needed to do, and he needed to do it fast so that Jenna didn't see this.

"Oh my God," came Jenna's whisper from immediately behind him. *Shoot. Too late.*

Ash turned and grabbed the doorknob.

"You don't need to see this," he said as he began to close the door.

"I've seen worse," Jenna replied as she slammed her palm against his chest, stopping him from shutting the door on her.

Her hand was hot and as strong as steel on his flesh. It was at that instant he realized that Jenna wasn't some prissy female who needed to toughen up. She was already tough. One had to be to not run out of this room screaming.

Reluctantly, Ash stepped aside.

"I saw the writing on the mirror. So, this must be Baby," Jenna said softly as she stepped into the room.

Ash was impressed that she wasn't shivering with revulsion at the sight because he was finding it difficult not to react. Instead, Jenna had a cautious smile on her face as she moved closer to the playpen.

Wow, this was the first time he'd seen her smile. Not a teasing smile. Not smug. Not sarcastic. But genuine and full of care. She looked nice when she grinned this way.

"Careful," Ash warned.

"I am," she replied.

Man, he wished he had just left the door closed and not come into this room. Wished they had never come here to this farmhouse. To find this here in the nursery. It was just sad.

"How old do you think it is...was?" Ash asked Jenna as he joined her and gazed down at the toddler walker.

"He was probably two years old. You are not a baby, anymore, are you?" she asked the bloated kid.

It growled at her and some slimy looking grey drool bubbled out of its mouth and dribbled along its blue bottom lip.

"Hey little fellow, I bet you've been stuck in there for long enough, wouldn't you say?" Jenna asked as she crouched just outside the playpen and gazed at the biter.

She had guts getting so close to the kid. Hell, he shouldn't even be thinking of it as a kid. It was an undead now and had Jenna not come in when she did, he would have taken it out already and been done with it. But Jenna seemed gentle and patient as she murmured sympathetically to it.

He hoped she understood that it should be put down. This was no longer human. Its skin was in sickly gray decomposition mode with strips of rotting flesh hanging off its face and other body parts and it didn't have any eyes left. It did have some nasty looking razor-sharp baby teeth though.

That would be the clack-clack sound he'd been hearing off and on, and the walker's teeth were snapping together hungrily as it stretched out its bloated arms at Jenna, acting just like a human toddler who wanted to be picked up.

He hoped she resisted the urge to do that.

"You know that nice big oak tree out back? The one with the tire swing hanging off the low branch?" she asked.

He wasn't sure if she was talking to him or to the biter.

"I think that would be a nice resting place for you and your parents," she said. "And maybe one more for your older sister? Or was she your babysitter?"

Oh, okay. Ash understood. She wanted graves dug. He didn't want to leave her here alone with it. She might do something stupid like pick it up.

"I think Uncle Ash here can go down and grab Uncle Tucker and have something waiting for you, so you can rest in peace, right Uncle Ash?"

Jesus. She was making him out to be a freaking uncle to an ankle biter. Was the woman nuts?

"I'll take care of it. That kid has a good set of cutters on him so be careful, Jenna."

"Ahh, I didn't think you cared?" She replied as she gazed up at him. There were cute little sparkles in her blue eyes and he wanted to say, I don't care, but he did. Too damned much. He realized that now.

"Just be careful. I'm already not in the mood to dig four graves for these deadheads and a fifth unnecessary grave would just piss me off and you don't want to piss me off."

He turned away and to his surprise, he heard her chuckle. Her laugh was sweet and light, almost like music. Something nice shifted inside his heart and suddenly he felt pretty good.

Yeah, she was going to be careful. She was a strong woman. He would make her *his* woman.

He left the nursery with a smile. It was the first smile he'd been toting for a woman in what seemed a hell of a long time.

Chapter Three

Jenna stared at the toddler and wondered why his parents had just left him here in the playpen. Had he died and turned while they'd been alive and they hadn't been able to put him down? Maybe they hadn't known how to do it? Or perhaps they'd killed themselves and hadn't been able to kill their baby and left him here in the playpen to starve to death?

Emotions welled inside of her as she slipped her saber out of its scabbard. Rick and one of his daughters would be walking around like this. Deadheads, searching for live prey. Hungry, drooling, stinking. They were probably still locked inside their apartment. She'd run out of there screaming, shutting the door behind her and she'd never gone back.

That Rick and Madison had been feeding off Addison meant she'd still been alive when they'd attacked her because, as Jenna had learned from Ash and Tucker, the undead did not attack their own.

That's why she had nightmares. Guilt about what had happened in that apartment. Had she stayed with the girls that night when they'd been down with the flu she might have been able to protect Addison. She wondered if Addison had known what had been happening to her? Had she seen her father come into the room? Had she trusted him, until he'd started biting her? Why hadn't Jenna heard the little girl cry out with pain?

Shit. Don't go there, Jenna. You dream about this shit almost every night. Keep it out of your day life.

The toddler in the playpen gurgled and kept reaching out to her, its teeth continuously chomping together as it stumbled against the restraints of the playpen. The child wore a dirty cloth diaper and that was it. He had brown hair, just like his parents, whom she'd put down just last night. Who knew how long they had all been locked away in this house. Hungry. Alone. Lonely?

Jenna punched away the sympathy that bubbled for this undead child and his family. She couldn't let emotions get in her way. This kid needed to be put down.

Slowly, she stood and tried hard not to let the cheerful look of the room distract her from what had to be done. She tried not to cry for what could have been a nice farm life for this family who lived near the U.S. and Canadian borders. She tried hard not to think about her own family who could be in a similar situation as she was in...surviving any way they could. Or in the same situation as this family? Undead? Yeah, she had to go home and find them and take care of her own kin. She wouldn't want them like this.

Jenna inhaled a sob, grabbed her saber, lifted it from the scabbard at her back, and brought the tip of the blade down into the child's skull. The honed end sliced through the skull easily and pierced the brain. The child fell silent and as she withdrew the saber, the undead toddler fell dead to the floor of the playpen. Now he would be at eternal peace.

Jenna slid her saber back into its casing and gazed down upon the little corpse. She wiped away her tears.

This life really sucks.

"Hey! Tuck! You down there?" Ash shouted into the darkness from the top of the stairs that led to the basement.

No answer.

Hmm, where was he? Ash had already checked outside but hadn't seen him. Earlier, Tucker had said he was going into the basement, and Ash hadn't seen him since.

Uneasiness rippled through him. Had Tucker met up with trouble down there? Should he get Jenna to cover his back while he looked? Nah, he could handle this himself. Besides, he didn't want her to think he was a chicken shit and afraid of going alone into the dark, spooky basement.

Oh boy, this sure was turning into one hell of a stressful day.

He flicked on his flashlight, decided not to use his knife, and instead removed his gun from the holster and began to descend. When he reached the bottom of the stairs, he stopped and listened.

Silence. As he aimed the light around and suddenly sensed something right beside him. Before he could so much as raise his gun, something hard clamped down over his shoulder.

Strong fingers dug into his flesh.

Shit! I'm dead!

"Boo!" came Tucker's shout, followed by laughter.

"Fucking asshole! I could have shot your head off!" Ash yelled as he wrenched away from Tucker's grasp. His heart just about pounded through his chest as adrenalin roared through him like a locomotive.

"Easy, my man. Geez, you sure do scare easy. I have a present for you. Check this out," Tucker said as he aimed his flashlight toward the floor near his feet.

Ash frowned when he noticed a cage. It was small, mostly made of plastic, with the front view consisting of small metal bars.

"What is it?"

"A pet carrier."

Ash shook his head.

"No shit, I mean what is in it? I see green eyes and black fur." He hoped Tucker didn't have a zombie baby locked up in that cage.

Tucker grabbed the handle and lifted the cage, allowing Ash to shine the light at the opening.

"Meow," came a pathetic cry.

"A freaking cat?" Ash couldn't believe it. Had Tucker found a cat? Even from here, he could hear it purring.

"Name is Baby. Says so right on his collar. It's a boy. Blue collar."

Shit. That message on the upstairs bedroom had to do with the cat. Not the kid.

"We can't take a cat with us. He would be too much trouble. How did it get in here anyways?" Ash asked.

"They have some contraption in a basement window where the cat can come in and go out through some swinging door. And why can't we take the cat? Jenna probably loves cats."

"Black cats are bad luck, man. Don't you know that? Let's get upstairs. We have graves to dig."

"I am not killing the cat!" Tucker spat.

Ash rolled his eyes. He really should let Tuck think a grave was for the cat. It would be a good payback for scaring the shit out of him.

"You're acting like a kid, Tuck. Grow up. Jenna had to take out a kid upstairs. Wants us to bury him and the parents and that other one out in the meadow. Wants them planted under that old oak tree. Since she is your woman, you should be doing all that domestic grave digging shit, not me." Ash taunted.

He turned and started up the stairs. He tried to ignore the creepy feeling of a hand slamming down on his shoulder again and he was very glad it didn't happen.

"Shit, really? You let her do that? Why didn't you do it?" Tucker growled angrily from behind him.

The accusation in Tucker's voice made guilt slice through Ash. He shouldn't have let Jenna do the deed. However, it was probably too late now. The least he could do was dig the graves.

"Because she didn't ask me to. Now come on. We have shit to do."

Several hot sunny hours had passed since they'd buried the farmhouse family. It had been sad to do it, but the cute little black cat had been worth all the trouble. To Jenna's amazement, she felt unusually calm as she leisurely stroked its soft black fur. She sat between a sleeping Tucker, and a quiet Ash, who drove them past the abandoned customs office, over the Thousand Islands bridge, and into Canada.

Despite it being very warm inside the truck, eerily creepy with no cars along the highway and no boats in the lakes, she was glad to be back in her home country. She was also apprehensive at what she might find at home. But she managed to avoid thinking about her probably dead brother and sister and parents, by taking care of the cat. She would deal with the bad when the time came. Right now, she had the kitty to think about.

Every time they made a pit stop, she carried the cat from the truck, fed him pieces of leftover rabbit and then brought him to a dirt area on the ground so he could attend to his business.

She was surprised that it wasn't afraid of being in the truck and that it didn't want to run away. Instead, he stuck to her like a dog, following her everywhere. She had no idea how long he'd been on his own but she knew in order to survive he must have caught mice for food.

He sure was an affectionate kitty and he never missed an opportunity to lick her face or gently nibble on her fingers and then curl up on her lap like a sleeping caterpillar. She loved listening to the melody of his crackling purr. Earlier, the rumbling noise had lulled her into a deep undisturbed nap and she'd awoken refreshed and happy.

She'd never had a cat in her life before, but the instant Tucker had presented this furbaby to her, she'd instantly fallen in love with him.

"Oxytocin, that's what it is," Ash said from beside her. She caught him wink at her.

"Excuse me?" she asked. What in the world was he muttering about?

"The cat. I once read that cats release oxytocin in humans. It's a hormone that is released when one is in love and you two are definitely in love."

"So you're jealous of a cat?" Irritation swept through her. Was this guy for real? Was he poking fun at her and her love for the furbaby?

"I noticed you've changed since we got the cat. He gives you affection and well, love heals all things."

"So, now you're a shrink?" What a dick head. It had only been a few hours since she'd gotten the cat and he was already being a dork.

He didn't say anything and from the firm set of his chin, Jenna realized he wasn't joking. She gazed down at the cat who was now looking up at her with his sparkling green eyes. His black whiskers twitched and her heart melted all over again. Gosh, the little guy was so cute. She resisted the urge to pick him up and let him lick her face again.

"You're not kidding, are you?" she finally asked.

"Of course, I am. Not," he said. He followed up that last word with a grin. She'd seen him smile before. A sarcastic grin or a teasing smile, both of which irritated her. However, this time she knew it was genuine.

Her tummy did a nice little flip and she suddenly realized she didn't want to leave these two guys at her first opportunity. At least not anymore. Quite the opposite. She wanted to get to know them more. A whole lot more.

"I swear that's the best damn dill pickle I have ever tasted," Jenna said as she chomped on her third crunchy pickle and moaned at the salty and sweet spices that tingled over her taste buds. Ever since Tucker had opened a jar of the farmhouse pickle preserve at supper and placed a pickle on her plate along with a couple of boiled potatoes, half a can of tuna, and some boiled vegetables, she'd been looking for any excuse to rob that particular Mason jar.

"You just make sure you leave some for the rest of us," Tucker said with a laugh.

Because they'd rarely seen a walker since turning onto the back roads, they'd decided it was safe enough to make camp at a secluded picnic area beside a small lake. It was nice to take a break from reality.

The scenery was serene and picturesque with the mirror-like water being a pretty blue and the nearby trees ablaze with autumn colors of red, yellow and orange. The sun was setting and it splashed a golden glow over Tucker who stood at the back of the black truck. He was shirtless and he gave her some knee-melting eye candy as bulging muscles jumped and twitched in his chest, biceps, and triceps while he washed the dishes on the slide out table that was usually stored beneath the doorway of the truck trailer. She'd happily given up her turn at dish duty with the promise of having sex with him tonight if he did the dishes instead. Not that she wouldn't have had sex with him anyway, but getting out of doing chores was kind of fun.

Ash remained quiet as he sat at the picnic table opposite of her and chewed on a piece of jerky. He'd taken several packages of jerky and other items from the convenience store they'd raided an hour earlier down the road. Thankfully they'd been able to fill some of their empty jerry cans and top up the truck's two gas tanks by siphoning gas from some of the abandoned cars in the parking lot.

"Where's that cat at? I have some beef jerky for him," Ash said with a sudden frown as he gazed around camp.

"In his cage, in the truck. I cracked the windows and put him down for the night," Jenna answered. That Ash was concerned about Baby's whereabouts was sweet.

"Thought you didn't care about him?" she asked. "That ruckus you put up back at the farmhouse saying the cat would only attract deadheads, made me think you'd be happy if he disappeared."

She caught him roll his eyes.

"Focus should always be on our survival, not on the cat. He's a distraction," Ash said.

"And you two men aren't a distraction?" The instant she said it she wished she'd hadn't. She noticed Ash tense. Saw Tucker gaze over at her.

"I mean..." Oh, dear. How was she going to change the subject?

"I mean by you guys finding these awesome pickles," Jenna said quickly.

"What exactly do you mean by a...distraction?" Ash prodded.

Darn. She should have known Ash wouldn't let this go.

"Yeah, Jenna. What do you mean by us being a distraction?" Tucker asked. He had come over from the truck and as he stood behind Ash he towel dried his hands.

She recognized the *I want sex look* splashed on Tucker's face and her breath literally went away as excitement roared through her.

When she gazed at Ash, he had a dark sensual expression on his face too. That both men obviously wanted to have sex with her tonight made a naughty hunger growl deep within her.

Their breathing had grown heavy and rough and their outdoorsy scents floated teasingly under her nostrils. She breathed them in.

Pine wafted off Ash. Tucker was scented with dish soap. The combination shouldn't have smelled so good. But it did.

"And you don't think that you are a distraction to us? Nibbling on those pickles with that succulent looking mouth of yours?" Tucker said as he stared with intent at her.

He continued.

"Don't you think I would love it if you would eat me alive, baby? Like you do to those pickles?".

Jenna's eyes widened at Tucker's words. He'd never spoken in such a suggestive way to her before. And he was doing it right here in front of Ash.

Nervousness and anticipation mingled within her.

Tucker had never proposed she...do *oral* to him. The thought of taking him *that* way hadn't even crossed her mind. The idea was tantalizing.

Tucker held out his hand and she instinctively took it. A moment later, he'd pulled her to her feet and she stood in front of him. He gazed at her as he continued to hold her hand. His other hand lifted and he brushed his knuckles softly against her cheek. It was an endearing gesture he'd done to her several times before.

"I knew this time would come eventually," Tucker muttered.

"What? What do you mean?" Her voice sounded hoarse and meek. She wasn't sure what he was saying.

"From here on out, you'll be having sex with both of us. Separately. Together. Whenever we want to take you, we'll take you," Tucker said. Although his voice was a whisper, his words were strong and dominating and her lower belly and pussy tightened with awareness.

She wasn't sure if she should protest, just for formality sake. The idea of submitting to their desires turned her on and it made her wonder if maybe her teasing Ash this morning had perhaps brought the men to this point?

"I have condoms," Ash said smoothly.

He was standing behind Tucker now, watching for a reaction from her. She looked at Ash's face and held his gaze. If he thought they were scaring her by saying both wanted sex with her, or if they were testing her in some way, she could give as good as they gave.

"Bring it on," she whispered. "As many condoms as you can burn through, I can keep up, if you can."

A low growl from Tucker made Jenna wonder if he was suddenly pissed off at her for flirting with Ash? But he kept gently caressing her cheek and didn't appear mad at all.

"She's a fucking tease and I for one will enjoy reigning her in," Tucker said in a firm voice.

Gosh, he sounded so damned sexy.

"Ash, you can take her as soon as we're finished here," Tucker suddenly said.

Ash nodded. His gaze flared with heat as he studied her for a long moment. Then there was a slight nod of his head. He turned and walked away.

Gosh, she loved the self-assured way Ash walked. His ass was plump and round against his tight jeans, and his stride was confident and easy going.

"Now you can concentrate on me, babe," Tucker said as pressed his finger to her chin and angled her face so her attention drew back to him.

"I know you want him bad, but I want you first."

She wanted to deny that she desired Ash, but she knew he would just see through the lie. Heck, if he was good with her having sex with two men, she was good with it too. More than good. As far as she was concerned there was no one left in society to judge her anyway and she loved this newfound freedom to explore her naughty side.

She just wished she knew why she was so attracted to a man who'd almost let her get taken down by a damned zombie?

"What? What's wrong?" Tucker whispered.

She reached up to curl her arms around his shoulders. Then she slid her hands against the base of his strong neck, brushing her fingers against his short velvety hair. She pulled him closer.

"It's nothing," she whispered back.

Liar! It was something.

"Come on, spit it out. You're frowning. Something's suddenly got you down. You don't want to get together with Ash?"

"It's not that...it's this morning was a close call with that walker. I'm pretty sure he saw it coming but waited until the last minute..." She should tell him she felt betrayed by Ash, but she didn't want to sound like a complainer.

"Shhhh," he said softly. He placed a finger on her lips, silencing her.

"We both saw it. Ash knew I had an arrow on the walker the entire time. Had you not moved fast enough, I would have taken it down before it got you. And you know I never miss, even from a far distance."

Confusion melted through Jenna.

"Then, why not warn me?"

"It was a test. To see how honed your skills have gotten since we've been together." Tucker chuckled as he whispered his finger back and forth over her lower lip. The gesture made her flesh tingle sweetly.

"Did I pass the test?" she asked. She wasn't sure if she should be happy or pissed.

"You're alive, aren't you?" Tucker replied with another chuckle. "You move fast, baby. Real fast. Don't lose that speed. Your awareness needs some working on, but you have the speed down pat."

"My awareness needs working on, eh?"

"Yeah, doll. Just keep practicing on following your instincts..."

"My instincts are telling me that you need me right now," she whispered.

"Right now?" he teased with a grin.

She enjoyed the hard contours of his body and loved the thick knot of his arousal as he pushed himself against her. They were belly to belly and her breasts were sensitive and heavy as she squished them against his chest. His hot hands slid up her back and he dipped his head. He took her lips full-on with strong possession.

Awareness rushed through her like a violent storm. Want buzzed and her blood boiled. She whimpered as his bold tongue thrust in and out of her mouth like a mini cock.

Pleasure and need coiled within her, pushing away her thoughts.

Impatience roared as she kissed Tucker. Her nostrils flared as she inhaled his man scent. She caressed her fingers through his short hair and kissed him harder. Erotic sounds rippled out of him and into her mouth.

He rocked his hips and his hard knot pressed intimately against her pussy. She undulated against him and moaned at the pleasure his bulge created. She glided her hands down his neck and smoothed them over his pulsing shoulders, loving the feel of his muscles as they rippled beneath her fingertips.

He slid his hands off her back, brought them around to her belly, then up and beneath her top, rising the cloth, allowing her breasts to spill free. He cupped her mounds in his palms, then dipped his head, and took a taut nipple into his mouth.

She gasped from the heat of his firm lips. Cried out as he gently nibbled on one aroused peak and then the other. He laved his bristly tongue over her sensitive flesh and then massaged her breasts with his fingers making her quake at the sweet sensations he created.

The wanton storm of need raged within and she kissed Tucker harder.

Suddenly there was another set of hands smoothing over her body. Hot and gentle hands. Ash had joined them. His fingers dipped beneath the waistband of her pants and panties. Within seconds he'd slid them down over her hips and knees. As her clothing puddled around her feet, she kicked them away. She was now fully naked from her waist down.

"I'll stay on guard duty. We'll have to take her one at a time until we get to a place that's safe," Ash muttered.

"In the meantime, here's a promise of things to come," he added.

She cried out with exquisite need as Ash pressed himself against her backside. He was naked and she trembled at the ultra-long outline of his hard cock as he pushed it against her ass cheeks.

Tucker broke the kiss allowing Jenna to catch her breath. But he had tensed. His body was rigid with awareness and she realized it was because there was no one on guard duty and that made them vulnerable to attack.

Tucker swore softly and Ash chuckled.

"Easy, Just wanted to tell you to bring her to the back of the truck when you're finished. I'll keep watch...and watch," Ash added the last word softly, teasingly. Then he slipped away.

Jenna's pussy felt heavy with need as Tucker settled his hands over her shoulders. There was a savage expression of arousal on his face. A heated look she'd never seen before. Fire and lust pulsed through her as he gently pushed her to her knees.

Within a moment he removed his jeans and underwear and his shaft was as rigid as a pole.

"Pickle time," Tucker whispered. He wrapped his hand around the base of his erection and his other hand slipped to the top of her head where he knotted his fingers into her strands. He held her head firm.

Jenna creamed as he pressed his thick erection against her lips. Heat cascaded off his flesh and caressed her face.

"Open, babe. Chew me like you do those pickles." His voice sounded hard and tortured.

Dutifully, she parted her lips and he slowly slid his cock into her mouth. He was big and his hot pulsing flesh stretched her lips. He almost touched her tonsils before he withdrew again.

"Suck me, sweetheart," he growled.

His fingers stiffened in her hair making sweet pain snap through her scalp. He thrust into her mouth again. She reached up and clamped her hand over his, and hollowed out her cheeks with an effort to create pressure.

He moaned. It appeared he liked what she was doing.

She squeezed her lips around his cock, savoring his flesh. He tightened his grip and forced her head to bob back and forth. She enjoyed the feel of the velvet steel as he slid in and out. The friction of his thrusts created a bruising heat that made her lips tingle.

As he fucked her mouth, she stared up at him. His eyes were scrunched tight, his cheeks appeared dark and his mouth was open as he panted. He truly was enjoying this!

"Awesome!" he snarled. "This.Is.Awesome."

He pistoned faster. Harder. She slurped and licked and kissed.

Suddenly he swore.

"I'm coming," he warned.

Suddenly spasms rocked him and he cried out. Hot jets spurt into her mouth and she quickly swallowed. Her lips danced around his shaft as she kept sucking and tasting and draining him. She loved the erotic sounds of his moans and groans and her pussy wept and clenched around empty air as she envisioned Tucker pistoning into her. She whimpered as he withdrew and cried out as he unexpectedly swept her into his arms.

"Now, it's Ash's turn," he whispered and then he carried her over to the truck where Ash waited.

Chapter Four

The air had gotten cool and the light autumn breeze felt nice on her heated body. It was almost completely dark now. The only light available was a white-blue glow from the bright full moon that rose behind the trees on the other side of the lake.

"I've been fantasizing about taking you since meeting you," Ash said quietly after Tucker set her down and then disappeared.

The knowledge that he'd been wanting her, intoxicated her. She'd thought he hadn't liked her and in return, she hadn't liked him either.

Until now, she'd been using him to teach her how to kill zombies and she'd been using Tucker for sex. Now she wanted Ash for sex too.

Her breath hitched as Ash slid his hands around her waist and he lifted her off her feet. It appeared he'd lain some bedding on the pull-out table as softness tucked against her ass when he set her there. Swiftly he grabbed beneath her knees and brought her close to the table's edge and she quickly kicked off her running shoes. Then he stepped in between her opened thighs.

He was breathing hard and muscles twitched nervously in his cheeks. His gaze lowered to her blouse, which had dropped to cover her breasts again.

"You look so beautiful, but this top has got to go," he whispered.

She smiled inwardly at his comment. He reached out and gently unbuttoned her blouse. Tenderly, he opened the garment and exposed her breasts. The tip of his tongue peeked out from between his lips as he slid the garment over her shoulders and down her arms.

Now she was completely nude and heated blood pumped through her as she looked down and spied his cock. It was ultra-long and interwoven with a web of bulging arteries and his rigid shaft speared straight out from his body. She expected him to thrust into her, but to her disappointment, he didn't. Instead, he cupped her breasts and dipped his head. He brushed her mouth ever so softly and she keened at the sweet impact.

His kiss made her light headed and knowing that Tucker was somewhere nearby watching was an erotic rush.

Forced by a need to touch his erection, she reached down and wrapped her hands around his wide girth. His shaft jerked between her palms and he groaned, ripping away his luscious mouth from hers.

"Bring me inside of you," he hissed. His voice was filled with tension and need.

"Condom?" she managed to breathe. The last thing she wanted was to get pregnant in this whacked out world of walkers. And he *had* mentioned condoms earlier.

"Hang on," he grumbled. He rummaged around in the bedding and then she heard the rip of foil.

"Give it to me," Jenna said softly.

"Better hurry. I need you bad," he growled.

Jenna smiled. "Makes two of us."

She eagerly accepted the condom and used the moonlight to slide the protection onto his engorged shaft. Then she wrapped her hands around his girth and pulled him forward until his giant cockhead pressed against her clenching vaginal opening.

"Take me," Jenna ordered.

She cried out and arched as Ash suddenly thrust into her. The fierce impalement brought a swift explosion of pleasure-pain. His shaft stretched tender muscles and he pierced her so profoundly she swore she'd never been penetrated this deep before.

He withdrew and as he entered her again, his mouth fused over hers, capturing her next cry as her pussy, hot and weepy, spasmed around his hot steel. She held tight to his massive shoulders as he began a wicked wild pistoning into her.

Pleasure-pain quickly flamed into waves of pleasure. Their harsh breaths ripped through the cool night air and the suctioning sound of their mating became a nighttime melody.

Ash's harsh mouth made love to hers. His velvet tongue thrust with confidence and his lush lips mated with hers until they were burning and tingling.

He kept thrusting. They were powerful strokes that stoked the storms of desire raging inside her. Her pleasure built and roared and soon she was embraced by tidal waves of sensations that dragged her into bliss.

Tucker stood nearby, hidden in the shadows. He'd hung his holstered gun from a tree branch right by his head, and set his crossbow and quiver of arrows against the tree trunk so he would have quick access to his weapons if any invited guests appeared.

In the meantime, his heart beat wildly as he took turns between watching Ash making love to Jenna and scanning their surroundings for walkers. He knew having sex out here in the open was the last thing they should be doing, but when it came to sensual pleasure, both he and Ash sometimes kind of lost their heads.

Although he felt relatively confident no rotters would come upon them out here far from any city or town, he also knew it was best to never assume. To assume meant death.

His mind wandered to their earlier conversation about how close that walker had gotten to her. He'd seen the betrayal and accusation flash in her eyes. He'd felt guilty about what he'd done to test her. But he'd squashed that guilt. Squashed it like a bug. She needed these types of tests. It was a crazy new world where only the strong would survive. She was strong, but he wanted her stronger. That was the only way she would be safe.

His breaths quickened as he listened to the soft sexy sounds of Jenna's whimpers and Ash's muted groans as their lovemaking grew frenzied.

The erotic scene of watching his friend taking Jenna had Tucker reaching down and wrapping his hands around his quickly re-stiffening cock. He stroked himself, using his fingernails to create the perfect amount of teasing friction along his steely flesh. His cock hardened quickly and as he pleasured himself he watched the two of them climax. Beneath the moonlight their bodies tensed and then Ash pistoned faster and faster until their muted cries filled the air and silence soon followed.

They'd already agreed earlier that he'd take first watch and then wake Ash to take over in three hours and then Ash would wake Jenna after another three. He watched as Ash lifted Jenna off the table and set her on her feet. They talked quietly for several minutes as they removed the bedding from the table and then slid the table back into place beneath the trailer. Then they climbed into the truck trailer and quietly closed the door.

He listened carefully to hear if they would have sex again, but no sounds came from the cab and Tucker felt utterly alone as he watched the white mist drift up from the dark lake. An owl hooted from somewhere far off and he tensed as something moved through the tall grass nearby.

But nothing appeared. Probably a raccoon or skunk or something small like that.

A few moments later the coolness of the evening had him shivering and he quickly donned his clothing. It was time to build a small, smokeless campfire and stay warm while he kept guard.

Jenna sobbed as she snuggled deeper into her sleeping bag. She'd taken refuge in a shed in the backyard of a house. The yard was well-fenced and would help prevent the walkers from getting in. There was a gate that allowed her to get out into a back alley that led to a nearby strip mall that had a grocery store. That's where she'd been getting her food.

Tonight, she'd grabbed a couple of cans of pasta and a can of mixed vegetables. She'd eaten the food cold, not wanting to start a fire to attract any looters or worse.

It was a cold June night and she'd bunked down early inside the shed. She'd been using the place off and on since the Apocalypse. She didn't spend the night in the same place more than once.

She was always on the move. Always making sure she wasn't followed.

She was so tired and scared she couldn't even think straight. All she wanted to do was cry all the time. Cry and hide from the increasing number of walkers that were showing up more and more on the streets.

It had already been three weeks since she'd left that apartment and abandoned Rick and the girls. The horror of what she'd witnessed there continued to haunt her, waking her in the dead of night.

Terrifying things were transpiring in society too. She'd gone to a couple of different police stations only to find them sealed. If she couldn't turn to the cops, then who could she turn to? She'd tried calling her parents from every phone booth she came across, but there were no dial tones. She'd managed to find a couple of cell phones, but nothing worked.

No phones. No electricity. No trains. No cars that she could start. No running water. Nothing.

There were walkers though. Many of them wandered the streets in a daze. Their mouths hung open, their teeth chomping up and down, making awful clattering sounds that got on her nerves. Their eyes were vacant, their bodies bloated, their skin sickly white or grey. Their stench overpowered Jenna to the point she wore a bandana over her nose and mouth. But it didn't help much.

She realized most of the living dead were trapped in their homes or apartments, having taken refuge there once they'd fallen ill. She could see the undead passing by the windows.

There were people too. Survivors. But they scattered away like mice when they saw her and she did the same with them.

Looters were everywhere. But there were no children. No elderly. The young and the old had all been wiped out. Had turned into rotters.

She'd learned quick too that she shouldn't trust anyone. One of her favorite horror tv shows dealt with zombies and she remembered what she needed to do in order to survive.

Trust no one.

So, she'd become a looter. A survivor. A loner.

What should she do? Leave the city and head north? Try to go home? But were her parents alive? Were her brother and sister alive?

She didn't know where to go. Didn't know how to get out of here. Didn't know if there would be food on the way.

Man. She was going to go nuts. She couldn't even make a damned decision.

A snapping branch broke her from her anxiety and Jenna stiffened in her sleeping bag. She'd lain small twigs and branches all around the yard as a security device. Someone or something had stepped on a branch. She lay motionless and listened.

Adrenalin screamed through her. Her heart pumped madly. Her mouth went dry as fear snapped through her.

Footsteps? Soft, carefully placed. A disturbance in the air just outside the shed? Was she just being paranoid? Or was someone standing right outside? There was no lock on the door. But she'd managed to place a couple of shovels against it. If someone opened the door, the shovels would fall over causing a commotion.

But the door didn't open.

Icy sweat blistered across Jenna's forehead. She wrapped her fingers around the saber she kept inside the sleeping bag with her. She held her breath. She waited.

"Hello inside the shed." A man's voice. Not too loud, but loud enough to freak her out.

Shit! She brought her weapon out of the bag and held it firm.

"Don't be afraid. We won't hurt you," came the man's voice.

We? As in how many were out there?

"If we wanted to hurt you, we could have taken you out last week when you were at Pop's Convenience store. Or at the pharmacy yesterday. Or at the grocery store earlier tonight."

Oh, dear God. She was dead meat sitting here.

"My name is Tucker. I'm here with my friend, Ash."

Go away! Please! Just go away!

She could hear the man breathing. Could hear a whisper. Then a soft knock on the steel shed door. The clatter just about made her pass out from sheer terror.

"Seriously, you don't need to be afraid. We wanted to let you know that we're here if you need us. If you want to talk. We're just around the corner. On Elm Street. #3. Okay?"

She dare not answer. Maybe they would think she wasn't here?

There was silence for a good long time. And then he spoke again.

"Okay. We'll leave. The offer stands."

Then she'd heard their soft footsteps fade away.

Her tummy rolled with nausea.

Holy smokes! She was going to be sick.

She grabbed a bucket she kept nearby and promptly puked up her supper.

After waiting a good hour, she packed her stuff into her knapsack and left the cold interior of the shed. She spent the rest of the night at another shed, in another backyard, barely able to sleep.

Someone knew she was here. Someone knew the places she frequented. She needed to leave this awful city. She should have left long ago. She should leave.

But she'd stayed, mainly because food began to appear at the doors of the places she hid.

The two men were stalking her. They were feeding her. She began to drop her defenses and when they finally showed themselves to her two weeks later, Jenna was terrified yet glad at the same time.

Instincts told her they'd been telling her the truth. They wouldn't hurt her. She would trust them. It was nice to have company. Wonderful to talk to someone again. She learned that their families were dead from the virus and both men came from Queens.

They began showing her how to kill the walkers and she felt power and confidence soar through her as she took out her enemies.

She would become strong. She would survive. Or she would die trying.

Ash came awake as he heard a soft moan from Jenna. His eyes popped only to find her deep in sleep beside him.

He'd been dreaming about last night. About making love to Jenna.

Man, he'd enjoyed the sex. Loved the way her eyes had scrunched tighter just before she'd come. He'd relished the clamp of her vaginal muscles around his hard cock when she'd orgasmed. The tension and spasms of her pussy massaging his shaft had rocked him to his very core and sent him spinning into his own release.

Yeah. He wanted to reach out and take her right now. But he didn't want to wake her. She was curled around him like a sexy vine. She was one warm lady. Everywhere she touched, his flesh felt oh-so-hot.

He remembered climbing into the cab and in the semi-darkness, she'd silently joined their sleeping bags making it double. Then she'd climbed in and he'd followed her. He'd spooned around her and they'd quickly fallen asleep.

Now her face was mere inches from his. Her luscious lips slightly parted and she had the most serene expression on her face.

Huh, he hadn't realized she had such long black eyelashes. Hadn't noticed the cute dark brown mole on the right side of her upper lip. Or that her eyebrows were so perfectly arched.

She was beautiful.

Ash stared at her for a long time before he realized it was actually very warm in here and quite bright. Sunshine streamed through a crack in the curtains and uneasiness and confusion whipped through him.

Why hadn't Tucker woken him? Why was Jenna still here? She would have been on sentry by now and Tucker should be asleep in here.

His gut hollowed out and his heart began a fast pace. Adrenalin shot through him like a lightning bolt. Had something happened to Tucker? Did a walker get him? Is that why he hadn't stuck to their planned routine?

He snapped his loaded gun from where he'd tucked it under his pillow last night and quietly released the safety catch. He should wake Jenna, but he didn't have the heart. She looked so peaceful. Man, he'd never seen her vulnerable side before and it was real nice to see.

Quietly he slipped on a pair of track pants that he had on a nearby hook and moved toward the rear of the trailer. He pulled aside the curtain on the door and anger burned through him at what he saw outside.

"How the hell come you didn't wake me up?" Ash complained as he joined Tucker at the picnic table a minute later. Anger continued to bubble and he hoped he could keep a lid on it because in not waking them up to take their turn at sentry duty Tucker had put their lives into danger.

His friend looked sleepy as hell as he stared bleary-eyed out across the glass-like lake. The sun was already high in the sky and they should have been on their way hours ago. Tucker's gun and crossbow were set on the picnic table behind him.

"Thought I'd pull an all-nighter. I can sleep while you and Jenna drive, and we can get back to the regular sentry routine tonight," Tucker replied as he grabbed his mug and sipped on his black coffee.

Ash's anger raised a notch.

"Hey man, we've discussed this before. You promised you would never pull an all-nighter again, especially after the last time..."

Tucker rolled his eyes and frowned. "I know, I know. I almost got us killed when I nodded off that time. But that was back in a city full of deadheads."

His voice softened as he nodded out to the serene sight.

"Cat likes it here. He's already caught and eaten three frogs. That guy is hungry and quite self-sufficient where his meals are concerned," Tucker said.

Ash noted the black cat quietly prowling along the lakeshore right in front of them. He also noticed the air was still and warm and not a ripple appeared on the blue lake.

"This place is too quiet. It's deceiving," Ash muttered. Over the months he'd gotten used to being alert and on edge. But this morning he'd woken ultra-relaxed and then discovering Tucker having screwed with their routine, he was now nervous.

He grabbed a mug off the picnic table and walked over to the small fire and lifted the metal teapot off the grill.

"I wasn't sleepy, until an hour or so ago," Tucker said. "Would have woke you up soon. Jenna still asleep?"

At the mention of Jenna, Ash immediately relaxed. He nodded as he scooped some instant coffee and poured the water.

"You're right about her. She is as sweet and addictive as sin," he admitted.

Tucker chuckled.

"And she makes a good bed warmer, too," Ash added.

"Yeah, I took a peek through a crack in the curtains earlier and noticed she'd intertwined herself with you like she does to me. I'm glad she was able to get a good night sleep."

Ash blinked in surprise. Usually, they would hear her whimper and cry out in her sleep or she would come awake in kill mode during a nightmare. But none of that had happened last night. Not a peep from her until just earlier.

It *had* been an unusually quiet, peaceful night. Excitement shot through him.

"Shit, you're right. She didn't make a sound and I slept like a freaking rock too. First good night I've had since this zombie apocalypse started."

Tucker grinned.

"You guys are good for each other. It looks like both of us may have to take her every night, just to ensure us all a good night sleep."

"I like the way you think, my man," Ash said as he returned the coffee pot back to the grill and joined Tucker at the picnic table.

They fell silent as they watched the cat chew on a long strand of grass. Suddenly its ears twitched and the cat's head snapped up. He was alert and staring to their left.

Ash tensed.

"Easy," Tucker said softly and nodded to their left where a couple of loons were flying low over the water. They splashed down on the other side of the lake and began to call out in their traditional mournful cries.

The cat stared at the loons and Ash relaxed.

"That cat might actually come in handy as a guard. All you have to do is watch the direction his ears are swinging."

Tucker nodded. "They say cats have great hearing. Why do you think I already knew the birds were coming in? I've been watching that cat for a couple of hours and I can tell you he's a pretty good guard. He hears things before I do."

Hmm, Tucker might have a point. Hell, they could use all the help they could get if they were going to survive in this nasty new world.

"What do you think happened here?" Jenna asked from beside Ash. Alarm etched her voice and her eyes were now as wide as saucers.

While she and Ash had taken turns driving all day, Tucker had slept with the cat snuggled in his arms. The cat's belly was obviously bloated, compliments of all those frogs he'd eaten for breakfast and the black furball hadn't so much as moved from Tucker's lap all day.

At the sound of Jenna's question, Tucker's eyes popped open and he joined them as they stared at the carnage in front of them.

Burned out buildings lined both sides of the street. Cars and trucks were overturned and blackened from fire. Whatever had happened here had happened fast and furious. The vehicles prevented them from driving through the downtown core of this city and Ash knew they would have to turn around and find another road to travel.

"Firebombed looks like. The authorities probably thought burning people alive would stop the spread of the virus," Tucker replied.

Ash had hoped Jenna wouldn't have to see such a violent scene but he knew he couldn't shield her. It was best to deal with reality as it unfolded.

"Gonna have to turn back and try another way," Ash said.

As he stared ahead he could easily make out the dark clouds of crows and vultures swirling in the skies along with the aura of flies that spun around each and every car or truck. Beyond the violent scene, Ash noted the bright early-October sun would soon disappear over the horizon.

They'd noticed the zombie population had been steadily increasing the closer they got to the Greater Toronto area and he knew it would be only a matter of time before any stragglers heard the rumble of the truck engine and began homing in on them.

Shit. He knew he should just tell Jenna that they should forget about going into Toronto to look for her parents. It was more than likely that city had been bombed too.

"I'm thinking if they survived, and heard about the bombings they would have cleared out of Toronto. Maybe they headed into the countryside where it might be safer," Tucker said.

This conversation about her parents most likely not being alive was one that they'd had with her many times over the recent days. Yet she'd insisted her parents, her sister or her brother would have left a note at each of their homes regarding their whereabouts. She'd also said she would go into the city alone and they didn't need to feel obligated to go in with her.

Man, he knew he shouldn't have made love to her last night. Knew he should have kept his distance, but now his body and his heart were involved. No way in hell was he going to let her go into Toronto on her own.

Jenna had remained silent as she nibbled her lower lip and stared out at the mess in front of them. He could only hope she would come to her senses, especially now with that cat involved. He held out hope she would not abandon the furball and head into the city.

"My cousin's house is about an hour north from here. We can go there for the night. If the house looks secure and they still keep the key in the same hiding place, then we can get in that way. It's not a large city and their place is a little out of the way on a large lake.

Hopefully, fewer walkers to deal with in a smaller town. Maybe my family went there," she said softly.

Well, shit. He was all for finding a safe place for the night. If it was safe.

She looked down at the cat that now stretched in Tucker's lap.

Ash was suddenly very thankful that Tucker and Jenna had wanted to keep it. It was kind of cute, but it was another mouth to feed. What the hell did cats eat besides frogs anyway? Didn't they need a proper diet? The next time he hit a store he'd look for some canned cat food.

He should remind Jenna too that everyone she knew was probably dead. That the flu virus had hit hard and fast. He'd seen it first hand. He'd gotten phone calls from his parents and his two siblings within days of each other saying they were seriously down with the flu. He'd tried to help each of them but they'd died, one after the other and he'd watched them rise again. He'd had to put them down. It had broke his heart each time. Yet killing them had made him strong. People didn't go through bad shit like that and not have it make them stronger.

Ash tightened his hands on the steering wheel as he gazed over at Tucker who gave Ash a slight nod to indicate that he was in agreement with Jenna.

"Okay, we go to your cousin's place for the night," Ash agreed. He doubted anyone would be alive there.

Without warning the cat hissed, jumped from Jenna's lap and dove under the front seat.

"What the hell is the matter with him?" Tucker snapped.

"What did you do to piss him off?" Jenna scolded.

"Nothing, he just fucking went nuts," Tucker snapped.

Walker! A warning screamed through Ash's mind.

Before he could react, something hard slammed against the side of the truck making all three of them curse.

Adrenalin and revulsion shot through him as a deadhead stared in at them. It was obvious the walker had been partially burned. Most of what was left of its clothing and flesh was charcoal colored. Grey drool streamed out of its lipless mouth and razor-sharp blackened teeth opened and closed in quick succession just like one of those wind-up toy chattering teeth.

Its burned palms were plastered against the closed window, and streaks of brown liquid dribbled down the glass. Even through the closed window, he could smell the stench of it. Could hear its sickening growls of hunger and rage.

"Fuck!" Tucker yelled as another one appeared at his window. It was just as burned, snarling and this one had no eyes. Pieces of black-burned flesh hung off its bloated face and neck.

"Okay, time to get the hell out of here!" Jenna's shout snapped Ash from his horror.

She already had her saber in hand and was shouting at Ash to get the lead out.

"I can't see out the side mirror cause of these deadheads," Ash complained. He couldn't see a freaking thing. He swore violently at the thought maybe they were being surrounded by a hoard.

"Go forward a few feet and try a tight turn," Jenna yelled.

A gun was dropped onto Ash's lap.

"It's loaded, safety is off, just in case," Tucker roared.

Ash took a quick look over at Tucker and noted he'd palmed his own gun and from the grim expression on his friend's face, he was ready to shoot his way out of the truck if need be.

Ash did what Jenna suggested and surged forward a few feet. Within a minute he had the truck turned around and he was weaving their vehicle between the lines of walkers who stumbled on the pavement toward them.

"Wooohoooo! Fifty points for each one you hit," Tucker suddenly shouted and then laughed.

"No hitting pedestrians. You'll lose your license," Jenna chuckled tightly.

Ash shook his head as he blew out a long tense breath.

Man, he wished he could just relax and joke around like these two idiots. But he couldn't loosen up. He had the feeling if he did, something bad would happen.

He pressed the gas pedal harder and made a quick dash down the street. Zombies were coming from every side street and all he could do was weave around their tattered bodies.

Jenna and Tucker continued with their joking and prodded Ash to hit a walker. But he couldn't do it. At least not intentionally. He'd only have to clean off the blood, guts, and gore and that wasn't a task any of them would enjoy.

To think that all these rotters had once been just like himself. Alive. It was unnerving to say the least. These run-ins with zombies kind of put life into focus. You just never knew if you would survive any one day.

Finally, there was one side street with no deadheads and he swerved the truck onto it. Before long he was on a highway free of walkers.

Man, that had been way too close. He was literally shaking and he knew without a doubt they'd dodged a bullet in getting out of there. He tensed when a few minutes later the cat crawled out from beneath the seat and jumped up on Jenna's lap.

He blew out a slow breath. He needed to de-stress.

He couldn't wait to get to this place Jenna had been talking about. Once it was secure, he would finally to be able to truly loosen up and relax.

Then he and Tucker could give Jenna a nice pleasure-filled night. He was really looking forward to something nice for a change.

Chapter Five

"House is secure," Tucker said as he entered the kitchen at the same time Jenna came up the stairs from the basement.

"Basement is clear too," she acknowledged.

She'd been on edge since seeing her cousin's house and wondered if maybe her cousin, aunt, and uncle walking dead inside. She hadn't been sure how she would react seeing them as undead. Probably end up screaming and never stopping.

But so far, so good. No one dead or alive inside this house.

They settled their gas lanterns onto the kitchen table and Tucker turned off one in order to save gas.

Relief finally sifted through her. For the first time since all this shit catastrophe had begun, she was in familiar surroundings and she felt relatively safe.

Everything looked much the same as the last time her brother, sister and herself had been here years ago the summer the before she'd headed off to college. A lot good that diploma did her when there was no more Internet, computers or a job.

This was a room trapped in time and she thanked God that no one had vandalized this little house on the lake. Aside from having to take out a couple of creepy walkers lurking around outside when they'd driven into the driveway, it appeared this house might truly be a haven from a world gone mad.

Jenna sighed as she settled her saber on the tabletop and gazed around the kitchen. She smiled as she remembered the old times when her brother, sister, cousin and herself had played games in here. Their parents' laughter would ring out when they got drunk on her uncle's homemade beer while they played cards out on the back screened porch or in the living room during their visits.

Life had been easy back then. Summer days filled with laughter while sunbathing on the sandy beach or swimming or boating in the lake a mere twenty feet from here. That would be followed by evenings outdoors roasting wieners or toasting marshmallows by a campfire and then nights here in the kitchen drinking Aunt June's homemade berry juice and eating her pies and cakes.

In the winter, during Christmas holidays, they'd visit her cousin, Cole and ice fish and rush the snow machines across the frozen lake and then come back inside and enjoy Aunt June's hot homemade vegetable soup.

And now all of it was gone.

Who the hell would have guessed a zombie apocalypse would screw up her world and that she would be one of the survivors. Many times, over the past months, she'd felt as if she'd been dumped into some kind of alternative world reality or maybe she was just lying in a coma after a subway accident and dreaming up all this shit.

A bright pink sheet of paper on the refrigerator door suddenly caught her attention. As she drew closer, shivers of disbelief screamed through her.

"Oh my God," Jenna whispered.

"What's the matter?" Tucker asked as he strolled up beside her. She pointed to the large, lone pink binder paper. Words had been written in a black marker and Jenna recognized her mother's handwriting.

Tears sprung to her eyes.

No way.

"Hey, it's addressed to you. Wow. This is unbelievable," Tucker said.

"What's unbelievable?" Ash asked as he walked into the kitchen.

She tried to ignore them as she read the note.

"The garage is secure. Cat is hungry and I for one am so hungry I could eat said cat," Ash said with a chuckle.

His joke about eating her cat should get him a sarcastic rebuff, but she ignored his taunt as she read the words.

My dearest Jenna,

We hope you are safe. Everything happened so fast. We tried to contact you many times but failed.

We are fine and we had to go further north to find a safer place. Do not stay here.

There are hoards. They come quickly and quietly. Please be careful, love.

I trust you remember how to find your uncle's friend's villa?

We love you. We miss you. Please hurry. I pray you are not dead.

Mom

The note was dated a couple of days after she'd run out of Rick's apartment. But by then the phones had been out and she'd realized very quickly there was a medical catastrophe taking place on a grand scale and she'd stayed away from everyone alive and dead, not wanting to catch the flu.

"They were here," Jenna whispered as she read the note again. Was she dreaming this?

"Who was here?" Ash asked.

Reluctantly she ripped her gaze from the note.

Ash had let the cat out of the cage, and it was on the table, purring and trying to nibble on a piece of beef jerky from Ash's hand.

That Ash was warming up to the cat should have made her ecstatic, but she was already there.

"They went up north. They survived. They're alive. It looks like all of them are alive. They're alive!" Happiness and disbelief rolled over her in such a huge uncontrollable wave that she couldn't stop herself from crying.

Tears blurred the note in front of her and heavy sobs of relief wrenched free from her.

"Hey, it's gonna be alright," Tucker soothed as he wrapped his arm around her waist and hugged her tight.

His warm embrace only made her cry harder. Only made her wipe madly at her tears so she could once again reread the note.

"Yeah, babe. This is awesome news. I am happy for you. Hell, I'm happy for all of us. Now we have a home to go to," Ash said as he moved in beside her and read the note.

Then he laughed.

"Fuck, it's a good thing we didn't go into Toronto. They left a damned note right here. Someplace they thought might be safe enough for you to see it. They must have figured you would eventually come here. Man, it looks like we're going to be alright, peeps," he said. His voice was thick with emotion and she swore his eyes were a bit brighter. Tears?

Home. Safety. Family.

This was just incredible.

"My parents. My brother. My sister. And my cousin, aunt, and uncle. They must all be alive. I cannot believe it. I really can't. I wish I could just pick up the phone and call them. I should have thought they might come here. Hell, we should have gone directly to the villa. Why wouldn't I even have thought of that place? They could easily convert it into a compound. It has walls to keep out the walkers. It has an old-fashioned pump with a well. It has an old outhouse. Backup generators."

"Doesn't sound like much of a villa. Where is this place?" Tucker asked with a frown.

"It's about a day's drive. Maybe less. We haven't been up there since I was a teenager. I'm not even sure exactly how to get there," Jenna sobbed. Goodness, she couldn't stop crying, no matter how hard she tried.

Panic shifted through her. Did she even remember the way?

Ash must have noticed her doubts.

"Hey, take it easy, we can find it," Ash reassured.

"Yeah, sure, we can find it," Tucker added. "You'll feel better after we eat. Food will get your brain cells remembering. And if food doesn't work...we have other ways," Tucker said with a wink.

Warmth flooded Jenna. Other ways meaning sex?

Oh my gosh! How could she even think about sex at a time like this? She wanted to hop into the truck and leave right now. But they were tired and they needed to rest. Heading out now would only put them in serious danger. Besides, she was hungry too.

"But we won't eat the cat. He isn't fat enough. Yet," Ash said.

Jenna laughed between her sobs and punched Ash's arm. His muscles were strong and she suddenly remembered last night. Remembered taking Tucker orally. The strength of his cock in her mouth. Remembered Ash's ultra-hard thrusts into her. Their moans as they'd climaxed together. Her ultimate satisfaction and the best sleep ever afterward.

Yeah, she would eat, but not so she could feel better. She'd eat because she'd need the energy to celebrate with the two men in her life.

Her family was alive and it was a miracle. She couldn't wait to see them again. Oh goodness, she was going to start crying again.

Two long-stemmed candles splashed enough of a glow over the kitchen area to allow them to eat their meal which consisted of canned meat, canned pasta, a jar of bean preserves and for dessert they'd had canned peaches and raw apples.

As Tucker leaned back in his chair he studied Ash and Jenna. They laughed as they watched the cat eagerly lap the condensed milk Ash had poured into a bowl on top of the table. Tucker and Ash had been pumping Jenna for any information she might remember about that villa that her mother had mentioned in the note. They'd even found a map of Ontario in a drawer and it appeared Jenna was pretty sure she remembered how to get there.

It would be another full day's ride to get to their destination and if they made it there alive, there might be some light at the end of this nightmare. Friendly people they could trust would sure be welcome.

Until they'd met up with Jenna, he and Ash had stayed away from any survivors. Early on, they'd had a couple of bad experiences getting robbed at gunpoint of the goods they'd pillaged from stores in New York City. They'd realized violent gangs of survivors were quickly forming and if they wanted to stay alive they would either have to give up their freedom and join a gang or keep their freedom and get the hell out of the city. They'd delayed their departure after spying Jenna sneaking out of a store one evening. They'd followed her and soon discovered she was on her own.

After gaining her trust, they'd told her of their plans and she'd suggested they travel north because she was going in search of her family.

And now here they were. Only a day away from Jenna realizing her dream. Tucker was so excited for her he swore he could bust from happiness.

Finding a note here from her mother was simply unbelievable and despite wanting to get the hell out right now and head up north, he knew the trek would be much more dangerous if they were not at their well-rested best. Today's almost misadventure in that fire-bombed city when the zombies had unexpectedly started showing up had shaken him to the core. Thanks to Ash's confident driving abilities, he'd felt safe quickly and had been able to join Jenna in having a little fun in teasing Ash to hit those walkers.

But right now, he had another kind of fun in mind. Something that would give all three of them a seriously good night of sleep. But sleep would come later. Much later.

Jenna stood at the railing of the small wood-planked square gazebo and gazed at the twinkling stars in the night sky. Her Uncle Merle had built the gazebo when he and Aunt June had purchased this house on the lake. He'd gotten a job as a prison guard at the penitentiary in the nearby town and they had moved out of Toronto taking away her favorite cousin, Cole. Jenna had been about five years old and heartbroken when Cole had left. She'd always looked forward to coming here and spending time with him.

That everyone had abandoned their homes for a safer place brought sadness to her heart. She'd never expected anything like this to happen in her lifetime. She wondered if this zombie virus was a worldwide phenomenon. It probably was. No one was coming to rescue them. No one would dare come, especially with it being most-likely contagious.

She inhaled and smelled the familiar soft scent of fish drift up from the lake. The gentle cool breeze made her shiver and she remembered it would be only a matter of days before the colder winds of autumn descended. Then would come the snow and a harsh winter.

She gazed down and smiled at the numerous initials etched into the white painted wood hand railing. Local friends had placed their initials here. Most of them, or maybe all of them were dead.

Oh man, this was ultra-depressing. She should go inside and climb into bed and have some hot and heavy sex with the guys. She enjoyed the pleasure she got from sex. Enjoyed the escape from reality. But she'd wanted to grab a few minutes out here and relive some old memories. After tonight, there was a good chance she would never see this place again.

If she listened hard enough, she could still hear her older brother Luke yell out in excitement that he'd caught a fish while fishing off the old dock, or her sister's hysterical screams as she'd raced out of the water having discovered a blood-sucker glued to her big toe. She could even hear Cole's gentle voice as he rhymed off the names of each and every plant that grew along the shoreline during their walks.

Days gone by. Never to be returned to her again. Only to be relived in memories.

She lifted her gaze and surveyed the lake. No lights twinkled from any of the houses or the cottages that lined the lakeshore. Every building was dark. Everybody was most likely dead or in hiding, afraid of letting themselves be seen.

Water rushed up onto the shore and from a nearby backyard of a neighboring house, she heard an owl hoot. Movement down on the beach caught her attention and Jenna made a move to grab her saber where she'd placed it upon the railing. But she opted to remain still and endure the stench of rotting flesh as a walker stumbled by just outside the wire fence. It didn't appear to know she was here and she wasn't in the mood to go outside the safe confines of the yard to deal with a deadhead.

Soon, it was gone and so was the stench.

If she never saw another walker in the next thousand lifetimes, it would be too soon.

She watched a small flock of squawking Canada geese as they flew low over the water. And there were gentle splashes and rings in the lake too where fish jumped out to grab a bug and then went down under again.

Wow. She'd forgotten how peaceful it could be out here in the north country. Forgotten how much she really had loved it here and at home with her parents. Why *had* she gone to New York to work? Money seemed so unimportant now. Family was the most important. She'd learned that when she thought they might be gone.

Was she being immature in thinking these thoughts about wanting to be with her mom and dad?

She shook her head. No, she wasn't immature. She was just dealing with reality.

Besides, had she not gone south of the border, she would never have met Ash and Tucker. Man, she did care for those guys. They had most likely saved her life. They had taught her things like strength, patience, to stay alert at all times and well...the sex was pretty good too.

Yeah, her guys were keepers.

"Here, I brought you a hoodie," Tucker whispered from behind her.

She swung around to find him at the bottom of the gazebo stairs and cursed herself for not hearing him approach. She really needed to practice honing her listening skills.

"Thanks," she said as a moment later he joined her. She slipped into the garment and was grateful for the warmth of the fleece.

He stood beside her at the gazebo and for many long minutes, they stared out at the lake. The full moon hung low and illuminated everything. The dock. The next-door neighbor's boathouse. The eerie silhouettes of overturned canoes nearby.

It was so quiet. But she could hear the rustle of the maple leaves and branches that towered above the gazebo as the wind blew a light breeze.

She could smell Tucker too. A soft scent of soap that made her realize he must have cleaned up after supper.

"Have you ever had sex in a gazebo?" he whispered.

Jenna laughed. "What? Are you fishing for information about boys I might have brought up here?"

His lips tilted into a sexy grin.

"Did you?" he prodded.

"Did I what?" She was hesitating. She wasn't about to tell him that she had never brought a guy here. That she wasn't all that much experienced in the ways of sex.

His eyes flared with excitement.

"Did you bring your boyfriends here? The gazebo is hidden way down here at the end of the property. A nice secluded spot to have a little fun."

He gave her a cute eyebrow wiggle.

"You're here. Do you count?" She asked as she turned to him.

"I'm not a boy," he answered in a guttural tone.

No, he sure wasn't.

Jenna's heart picked up speed as he twisted around to face her. Lust shone brightly in his eyes.

"Show me that you aren't a boy," she teased.

He cursed softly as she reached out and placed her hands on his chest. Heat greeted her fingers and his muscles flexed and jumped beneath his track top. She could feel his heart pound and hear his breathing quicken.

He reached up and tangled his fingers in her hair. Suddenly it was as if he filled the entire gazebo. He was a big guy. Tender yet tough.

His facial features softened in the moonlight. She noted the dark beard stubble on his face. The sexy tilt to his lips.

"Have I told you lately how beautiful you are?" he asked with a softness in his voice she'd not heard before.

She reeled from his confession. Wow, that had come right out of right field.

"Actually, I...I think this is the first time you've told me that," she whispered.

"Even if I haven't said it out loud, I have been thinking it."

"You have?"

"I have, sweetness."

Her tummy did some mighty nice flips as his head lowered. She closed her eyes as his mouth brushed playful featherlight touches against her mouth.

She tasted his lips. They were scented with mint toothpaste.

"Mmm, you taste good," she whispered.

"I bet you taste good too, but I'll find out later." She wondered what he meant by that, but her thoughts were fried by fire as his mouth suddenly melted over hers. This kiss was hard and possessive and left no doubt in her mind that she belonged to him.

He ravaged her mouth. Each stroke of his lips created flames of want inside of her. Every sexy moan that escaped him made her heart pound this much faster. Heat surged through her.

She wanted him to take her here. Now.

She slid her hands off his chest and found the hem of his track top. She nudged his top upward and he quickly broke the intoxicating kiss, grabbed his clothing from her and yanked his top over his head and off. He bunched it and tossed it over the railing.

Then he turned to her revealing those lovely corded muscles in his shoulders and across his chest.

He was panting now and he helped her out of her hoodie and then out of her shirt. She wore no bra, so her breasts spilled free and he quickly palmed them in his hot big hands.

She was conscious of the chilly air floating against her back, but warmth cascaded off his body to keep her front nice and toasty.

"Ash is waiting for us in one of the bedrooms. I was supposed to come out and get you. He is probably watching us. Just like I was watching you two last night," he breathed as he slid his hot hands against her waist.

"You're a sexy peeping Tom. Did you enjoy the show?" she asked.

A naughty tingle of excitement rippled through her imagining Tucker hiding in the shadows while Ash made love to her.

"Watching you two kept me hard all night," he muttered. He gave her an erotic pout.

Jenna chuckled. She slapped her hands upon his sleek chest and trailed her fingers over the banded muscles. His breathing grew quicker.

In a second, she found each of his nipples.

Right now she didn't want to think about Ash. She just wanted to taste Tucker.

She leaned closer to him and drew his left nipple into her mouth and suckled.

"Woman, what are you doing?" he gasped and jerked.

He liked it. She could tell in the way his hips gyrated and he pressed himself against her. His erection was hard and big, an undeniable proof that he was aroused.

"Making love to your nipple," she muttered. She then took the hot bead deeper into her mouth. Maybe it was her imagination, but she swore his nipple hardened and got bigger as she nibbled and sucked.

She moved to his other nipple, teasing it with intimate pulls and naughty nibbles and the guttural sexy sounds he made, made her heart so happy.

Having Jenna's seductive mouth upon his nipple just about brought Tucker to his knees. Man, what was possessing this woman tonight? She wasn't usually this bold. It was like she was out of control and she was making him join her very quickly.

Her mouth slid from his nipple and she stroked her tongue over his chest muscles. Each lick was a lash of fire. Each kiss a brand of ownership.

Heat roared through him and his cock hardened into a molten spike of need. He gasped as she moved her mouth onto his sensitive nipple again. Cried out as she bit his tender flesh.

He loved the softness of her fingertips as they explored his muscles. Could feel perspiration shimmer over his forehead as his body blazed with arousal. He remembered last night when she'd taken his cock into her mouth. The tight fit of her lips around his shaft. The intimate way she'd milked him dry as he'd orgasmed.

The desire to take her right here and now raged. He couldn't remember being so hot for a woman before. She smelled like sunshine and moonlight and flowers. She smelled like life.

He couldn't get enough of inhaling her scent. But suddenly another smell intruded.

Damn! He'd forgotten they were outside. He wasn't even sure if the wire fences were secure. He hadn't taken the time to check. Time to head indoors. He gazed over her shoulder just in time to see two figures emerge from the lake.

Frig!

Alarm rippled through Tucker and she yelped in surprise as he suddenly he swept her up into his arms.

"What?" she whispered. Alarm made her eyes bright.

"Taking this inside," he answered.

No use in totally ruining the mood and telling her he'd just spotted a couple of walkers stumbling out of the lake. He wondered how many more were out there. Her mother's note had mentioned hoards and not to stick around here. He needed to get her into the house. To safety.

As he walked up the stone pathway toward the back of the house, he spotted the flutter of the drapes at a bedroom window.

Ash had been watching them. He'd know she was primed and ready. They could take her together.

Oh man, he needed her bad tonight. Real bad. He was hard and hurting.

Tucker picked up speed.

Her hands were like hot brands on his naked shoulders as she reached out to hold him.

"My saber..."

"Tomorrow. I'll pick it and our clothes up in the morning. It's not like someone is going to steal our stuff," he said softly.

At least he hoped not because he thought she looked sexy swinging that blade and lopping off heads of walkers.

She smiled and he sucked in his breath as she cuddled against him. Soft curves melted against his body making him wonder how much more of this sensual torture he could take before he lost his self-control and just took her right here on the pathway.

The seductive caress of her warm breath spurned him to move faster. He ascended the stairs in he bet faster than anyone had ever taken these creaky wooden stairs. Then he had her turn the doorknob on the door. He entered the screened porch, kicked the door shut and then moved quickly into the house.

"Enjoying yourselves without me? You wound my heart." Ash said with a strangled chuckle, a moment later, when Tucker stepped into the bedroom and set Jenna upon her feet.

Due to several candles flickering on a nearby bureau, Tucker could easily see that Ash wore only his underwear and the front of it was tented from his bold erection. Yep, he'd been watching them.

"Entertain her. I'll make sure the doors and all windows are secure. Be back in a sec," Tucker said.

Man, he couldn't believe his survival instincts kept working even during a sensual time like this.

"I already took care of everything. Cat is asleep in his cage. Just lock the back door and in the meantime, I'll keep this lovely lady nice and warm."

Tucker grunted as he heard Jenna moan. Before he left the bedroom, he saw Ash cup her breasts and lower his head to attach his mouth to one of her plump nipples.

Tucker grew harder than he'd ever been in his life at the erotic sight. He almost stumbled in his hurry as he walked down the hall toward the back door.

Man, he had a gorgeous red-haired woman that needed some hot loving and he had to think about locking the freaking door? Wasn't like they were going to be disturbed. Everyone and their mother around these parts was undead walking.

He should have his head examined. Hurriedly, he locked the door.

As Ash sucked on Jenna's luscious nipple and listened to her gasps of arousal, time seemed to stop. All he could do was feel. Feel his heart pound, his cock harden and his lips tingle around her hot throbbing flesh. Her hands had settled on his waist like two hot brands and he shuddered as she gently rubbed and nudged her knee against his ultra-sensitive shaft. He could easily come if he allowed himself to.

So. Damned. Easily.

"Ash," she said quietly. Her voice was strained, filled with need. Her breaths raspy and fast.

He stiffened as her hands slid off his waist and she trailed her fingers beneath the waistband of his underwear. She wrapped her hands around his shaft so quickly, he didn't even realize how it had happened.

But she held his cock as if it were precious cargo and he quickly realized the power she had over him as she began a sultry squeeze of his rigid flesh. Then she drew her nails over his shaft.

"Keep sucking," she whispered in a hoarse voice.

He hadn't realized he'd stopped!

He took her pert nipple into his mouth again and drew and plucked until she was moaning. Then Tucker was beside him. He didn't say a word as he settled beside Ash and then drew her other nipple into his mouth.

She jerked and whimpered as they both made love to her nipples. Yeah, he could stay here all night long at her sweet breast. Maybe forever.

Chapter Six

Every nerve inside of Jenna was zinging with pleasure at having two men at her breasts. Hot lips sucked on her tender nipples making her knees weak and making her feel as helpless as a newborn lamb as she tumbled within pleasure.

Calloused hands kneaded her breasts, and confident palms caressed her belly.

She moaned and cried out as their sucks grew rougher. Beard bristles sparkled friction over her flesh and their masculine heat pummelled her.

She needed to get out of her pants. Needed to be penetrated. Claimed.

Suddenly their mouths left her and she was being lifted into the air. She wasn't sure who picked her up because her eyes were so heavy-lidded, she struggled to open them, so she could see.

She was gently laid out on the bed, and her shoes, socks, panties, and pants were quickly removed. She cried out with surprise as someone grabbed her by her ankles and pulled her further down the bed.

"Lift your ass," Tucker instructed in a thick voice.

She did as he asked and a small pillow was shoved beneath her butt. Her legs were spread wide and suddenly her eyes had no problem popping open as curiosity washed over her.

She discovered Tucker standing at the foot of the bed and he stared down between her thighs. His expression was hard with arousal. His eyes darkened with lust. The pink tip of his tongue peeked out of his mouth as he stroked his shaft. It was long and erect. His body looked tense and muscles jerked in his arms and chest.

The mattress moved as Ash stretched out on the bed beside her. He rolled onto his side and faced her. His body heat branded her and perspiration whispered across her forehead.

"Hey sugar," Ash breathed.

He reached out and touched her chin with his thumb and forefinger. He tilted her head so that she faced him.

Goodness, he looked so handsome. In the glow of the candlelight his gaze appeared hungry and lustful, and his teeth flashed white as he smiled at her.

She reached over and touched his face. Her fingertips explored the bristly beard on his chin and cheeks and traced the plump outline of his lips.

When the mattress dipped between her legs, she wanted to see what Tucker was up to, but Ash's soft voice stopped her.

"Don't look down, baby. Just feel," he murmured.

She whimpered and closed her eyes as Ash's lips danced over her mouth making her brain short-circuit. She moaned as Tucker's shoulders nudged her legs farther apart and his hot breath blew against her clitoris.

Ash moved a hand over her belly, his palm sliding back and forth over her skin in an erotic rhythm.

Fire lanced her as a tongue swiped between her pussy lips and she trembled at Tucker's sensual touch. His tongue swept around her clit making her arch her hips.

"Oh yes, this..." she purred. She enjoyed the intimate way Tucker licked her pussy.

She tightened her thighs against his shoulders. Her breathing quickened.

Lips licked and kissed and hands explored and touched until she was suspended on a wonderful rack of pleasure and every nerve ending in her body became sensitive to their every touch.

Suddenly Ash was leaving her. Her eyes popped open and she watched him move over her, his torso angling over her face. His shaft, long and rigid mere inches from her face.

She opened her mouth and his swollen cock pressed against her lips. He was breathing harshly as he thrust the head of his erection in. She tightened her lips around Ash's flesh and she moaned and bucked as a couple of Tucker's fingers slipped into her vagina.

The silky solid feel of his pistoning power made Jenna eager to please. She sucked and licked and slurped at his flesh as he moved in and out, bruising her lips. She heard Ash praising her. Heard his moans and groans as she loved him with her mouth.

He thrust in rhythm with Tucker's fingers. Steady, deep and oh so penetrating.

Her mouth squeezed, her pussy tightened.

She panted as she struggled to keep up with Ash's thrusts. She bucked as Tucker's fingers impaled her and then he withdrew only to penetrate her again, fast and furious.

Sensations swamped her. Lust tore through her and everything exploded.

Her mind. Her body. Her soul.

Wave after wave came the pleasure. She convulsed around Tucker. Bucked and writhed and then groaned around Ash's erection.

Exquisite shudders raced through her. Embraced her. Made love to her.

She jerked and spasmed. Their driving strokes pushed into her body. Firmer, quicker until erotic vibrations roared through every part of her.

The firestorm continued. She didn't know for how long she rolled within the pleasure, but perspiration drenched her and shudders flamed through her.

As her orgasm ebbed, Ash warned her that he was coming. He withdrew and then he was leaving her. She barely spied him spurting into a nearby towel before Tucker was moving over her.

His big body came down on top of her. His long, thick shaft plunged deep inside of her and his mouth melted over hers in a mind-shattering kiss.

Jenna climaxed again. Her vagina tightened around Tucker's solid flesh as she spiraled within the shudders.

Tucker withdrew and pistoned into her.

She spasmed and cried out and became wonderfully lost within the pleasure once again.

"LOOKS SECURE ENOUGH," Ash said from beside Jenna, as the three of them, along with the curious cat, sat in the truck and stared at the villa in front of them.

She thrust the truck into park and as her heart pounded insanely against her chest she stared at the place, eagerly searching for any sign of life.

Jenna couldn't believe she was actually here.

The place looked the same. More unkempt than she remembered, but one didn't go out and cut the lawn in the middle of a catastrophe. There was the same black wrought iron-barred fence of about ten feet high that lined the entire front of the property and she remembered that the fence surrounded the entire grounds.

High bushes and other greenery hid a good part of the front of the house. But she could easily make out the two top floors of the three-story white wood-planked Gothic-like house with fancy mansard roof. She'd always loved the architecture of the roof with its four sloping sides, each side becoming steeper halfway down and had spent many an hour admiring it in the past.

"Shit, that's one big mother of a house," Tucker muttered from beside her.

"Several balconies, turrets, and plenty of fancy windows for sentry duty and defense," Jenna answered. This would be a good fortress against a hoard attack. Hopefully, they would never have to endure one, but she had the feeling what they'd experienced with those zombies the other day in that burnt out city was probably something similar to what a hoard would be.

"I forgot how big this house is. It's a century home turned into a bed and breakfast. They call it The Villa." Jenna said. She pointed to the elegant and colorful sign to the left of the gate.

Welcome to The Villa Bed and Breakfast Century Home.

"How can we get in? The front gate is chained and padlocked and the spears at the top of the fence might impale things I don't want impaled," Ash said with a chuckle.

Suddenly the cat jumped off the dash and scurried beneath the front seat.

Shit. Jenna went for her saber.

"Heads up, zombie alert," Tucker said from beside her. Both Ash and Tucker reached for their guns and Jenna eagerly searched what she could see of the grounds to see if anyone was even here.

Her tummy hollowed out as a sudden idea hit her. Maybe her family hadn't made it here after all? Maybe they'd run into zombies and were now dead?

Don't go there, Jenna. Stay positive or you'll snap!

The place looked abandoned and disappointment rocked through her big time.

"I'll take care of it," Jenna said and stepped out of the truck to meet the butt-ugly looking bloated zombie that was ambling toward them.

It appeared to be an older person. A tall man. Its clothing was tattered, its skin deathly grey. Strips of blackened flesh hung from its face and its temples were sunken in. It had no eyes and no nose, just black hollow areas, but its lipless mouth was full of nasty looking teeth that chomped up and down as it stumbled toward her.

The undead son of a bitch thought she was going to be tonight's supper, did it?

"Fuck you!" she yelled at the walking corpse.

Anger flowed through her. This was not the time to be slaying zombies! She wanted to see her family!

She heard Tucker and Ash curse as they stepped out of the truck. She hoped they would remember to shut the truck door so the cat wouldn't get out. But she didn't have time to remind them. The walker was looming closer and it smelled foul.

Damn, she hated the smell of rotting flesh.

Jenna stepped forward and with one wide swing of her saber, she sliced the blade right across the neck of the walker. With a woosh, the head flew off, and the body dropped. Without hesitation, she stepped toward the head and stabbed the sharp metal into the skull. Its creepy, drooling mouth stopped moving.

"Good job, sis," came a familiar voice from immediately in front of her. Jenna's head snapped up to see her brother step out from behind a tall clump of bushes and into the opening.

Tucker and Ash were in crouched positions in front of the truck and they were aiming their guns at her brother. He stood on the other side of the fence, a rifle in each of his hands and the weapons pointed directly at the guys.

"Luke!" she shouted. She was so glad to see him.

"Tell me now if I need to shoot these two, Jenna," Luke barked.

His voice was stern and his face determined. She had no doubt he would start shooting if she told him to.

"Luke! Oh my God! No, don't shoot them. They're with me!" she shrieked as fear pummelled her.

Her brother looked different. His dark brown hair was shoulder length and unkempt and his gaze was hard and determined. Dark shadows hung beneath his eyes and a five o'clock bristle hugged his cheeks and chin.

"Then tell them to ease down their weapons and step away from them," Luke said tightly. Muscles twitched in his cheeks.

She swore she could feel the tension sizzle through the air between her brother and Ash and Tucker.

My God, she hadn't expected this type of aggression from Luke. He'd always been so friendly, easy going and full of joy. But now he looked serious and deadly.

She trembled as she slowly placed her saber onto the grass in front of her and then backed away.

"Easy, take it easy, bro. I can vouch for them. They're my friends and they've kept me safe all the way here," she reassured.

Ash and Tucker didn't say a word as they stared at her brother. Wow, if looks could kill, there would be a shootout going on here now.

Tremors of uneasiness shot through her. Why was everyone acting so damned over cautious?

"Guys? Can we chill? Please?" She begged.

She knew Ash and Tucker would feel vulnerable without a weapon. Hell, she didn't feel like dropping her weapon either, but she had.

"We're not giving up the guns. For all we know, he could be part of a gang now. People change, Jenna, especially after what we've all gone through!" Tucker growled.

He looked more pissed off than she'd ever seen him. Ash appeared quite angry himself.

A bad feeling slithered through Jenna as she eyed Luke. Had he turned against her? Were there bad men inside the house? Had he and her family joined some sort of gang?

"No gangs here. Just a lot of guns. And they are all trained on these strangers," Luke said in a cold voice. Despite the late afternoon sunshine splashing on her, she felt chilled.

"They are not strangers!" she yelled.

Fuck!

"Stand down, Luke!" A familiar voice shouted.

Jenna couldn't believe her eyes as her father, rifle in hand, stood at the gate. Where had he come from?

Happiness burst through her and before she knew it, she was running to where her dad stood smiling. Her legs just about gave out as she rushed up the driveway to the gate and thrust her hands between the bars.

"Pappi! Oh my God! I am so happy to see you!"

Her dad grabbed her fingers and squeezed tight.

"Hey, love. I told mom, you would make it. I told her to have faith. Now come on. Come inside."

Reluctantly she let go of his hands.

Her thoughts whirled as he thrust a key into the padlock. It opened and her dad began to unravel the steel chain that held the gate closed.

"All of you, come inside," her father said.

As he swung open the gate she flew into his strong arms. She was home!

"That was the best food I have ever tasted, Aunt June," Jenna complimented. They'd been here only a couple of hours and she felt as if she'd never been apart from her family.

Everyone had survived the flu. Well, actually not everyone. The owner of this house and his wife were walkers. When her family had arrived here, they'd opened the front door and Mr. and Mrs. Smythe had wandered out and tried to attack them.

No one had had the heart to take them down, but they'd managed to lure them off the property and they hadn't been seen since.

"I swear you have lost so much weight, Jenna. And I aim to put it right back on you again," her Aunt June said as she clasped her hands to her chest and stared at Jenna and then at Tucker and Ash who sat at the table at each side of Jenna.

"You boys need to put on more weight too. You need to be strong to fight those zombies. Can I get you boys more supper?" Aunt June asked.

Boys? Jenna almost burst out laughing.

"No, thanks. I am stuffed," Ash mumbled as he shoved another forkful of carrot salad into his mouth.

"I'm good. Thanks so much," Tucker replied. He sat back in his seat and patted his stomach.

"I'll get started on the dishes then," Aunt June said.

"I'll help you and then I need to get back on guard," her brother said. He glowered at Tucker and Ash and then followed Aunt June out of the dining room.

Jenna's mom laughed. "Don't worry, boys. Luke will warm up to you. He's taken the job of keeping this family safe to the extreme."

"Better safe than sorry," Ash said with a smile.

Her mom nodded.

"He's been quite uptight too since he lost his wife to the virus," her mom added. "I worry about him."

Sadness whipped through Jenna. She'd noticed almost immediately that someone was missing and now understood why Luke had changed. Beth was dead.

But she didn't want to dwell on the dead. She wanted to be happy. To be grateful for what she had.

Jenna couldn't get enough of looking at her mom. She appeared a little older than the last time she'd seen her last Christmas. There were more streaks of white in her hair and more wrinkles on her face.

But she was alive and that's all that mattered.

"Who wants a beer?" her dad suddenly asked.

There was a happy chorus of agreement from her cousin Cole, her uncle, and Tucker and Ash.

"Okay, gentlemen. Come on into the living room and sit and drink with me. I've got a deck of cards all ready. We can let the ladies catch up on things," her dad said. He turned to Jenna and gave her a warm wink.

Thanks, Dad, she mouthed the words to him as the guys left the room amidst a sudden robust conversation that was started when her uncle asked if anyone wanted to go hunting for deer with him early in the morning.

Jenna sighed in relief. She would finally have some alone time with her mom and her sister, Janna.

"Typical men, eh? They like their beer," Janna chuckled as she lit up a cigarette.

"Hey, I thought you gave up smoking?" Jenna asked. She always hated that her sister had picked up such a bad habit at an early age, but she'd loved it when Janna gave up smoking a couple of years ago.

Janna shook her head and sucked in a deep drag. The end of the cigarette glowed bright orange and then she blew out a bunch of perfect smoke rings.

"Yeah, well, Jenna, try staying off cigs when the entire world goes into zombie land and you get cut off the Internet."

Jenna laughed.

"You have a point," she said.

"So, love, where in the world did you pick up those two men? They are adorable and so well-behaved," her mother said, as she grabbed Jenna's hand and squeezed her fingers.

Well behaved? Wow, if mom only knew what her so-called well-behaved men had been doing with her daughter.

"Long story, mom. But they've been really good to me. They took me under their wing. They taught me how to fight and how to kill. And how to survive."

Her mother smiled and her blue eyes twinkled with sympathy.

"I can see in your eyes that you have been through hell, my darling. But now you're safe here. Back with your family. We'll take care of you. We will take care of each other," she squeezed Jenna's fingers again.

"So which one of those men are yours?" Janna suddenly asked as she leaned forward, interest quite blatant in her blue eyes.

"Actually, they are both mine. You best keep your hands off them," Jenna blurted.

Her mother gasped at Jenna's bold answer and Janna's mouth dropped open in shock.

Jenna had never experienced the feeling of jealousy before, but possessiveness was running through her veins now.

She may as well stake her claim on Tucker and Ash right here or her sister would dig her claws into one or both of them. Janna was older than her by three years and worldly in the ways of sex. She even had her own explicit Internet show with thousands of members who paid her monthly fees to see her naked and playing with sex toys. But Janna had never told her parents about her job. They thought her sister was a well-paid hostess at a fancy restaurant.

Jenna had never told their mother about her oldest daughter's secret naughty escapades. She wasn't about to now, but Janna would know that that threat was hanging over her head, so she would back off Jenna's men.

"Wow, you lucked out, baby sister. Don't let dad know or he'll have their asses out on that camper truck the three of you came in on."

"Then there will be three of us leaving together, just like we came in." Jenna snapped. She held her head high and felt proud that she was able to stand up to her sister.

"Now, now, daughters," her mother's soft voice calmed Jenna's momentary anger. "No one is leaving and no one is fighting. Jenna is old enough to make her own decisions where her men are concerned."

Jenna blinked in shock. Her prim and proper mom, who had always told Jenna and Janna to behave like ladies around men, and never spread their legs unless they had a wedding ring on their finger was now telling Jenna she could do whatever she wanted under this roof?

"Give me a hug, sweetheart. I have missed you so much," her mom said. She held out her arms to her.

Jenna didn't waste a second and swept her arms around her mother. It felt so wonderful to be in her mom's warm and welcome embrace.

She had been hugged off and on by everyone since she'd arrived here. And she knew the hugs wouldn't end. Not ever.

Home was where her family was, so she was home. She was safe.

She was loved.

The End

Spunky Girl Publishing Mini Catalog

~ Jan Springer ~ Erotic Romance ~

Shades of Ménage Box Set
Contains 4 books! Jude Outlaw, The Claiming, Perfect and Imperfect.
The Outlaw brothers are returning from the Terrorist Wars to Claim
their women...Jude Outlaw & The Claiming, Books 1 and 2 in the
Outlaw Lovers series.

A fast-acting virus has been unleashed, killing a vast majority of the world's female population, forcing the introduction of the Claiming Law. A law that states women are property that can only be claimed by groups of men...

This boxed set also includes "Perfect" and "Imperfect". Environmental contamination has made the world unlivable. The sick outnumbers the healthy. Hospitals are overwhelmed. Economies collapse. Governments combine to form a one world power called the "Order of Authority"(OA).

To save the human race the OA builds "biospheres"—large bubbles enclosing self-sustainable cities. Only the healthy are allowed inside. Everyone else is left to die...For population control, each human is embedded with a microchip, suppressing the urge to mate. The art of lovemaking vanishes...

Centuries later...

A rebel group of young doctors are secretly tampering with their microchips and experimenting with intimacy. Now they search for allies who can help them with their cause – to eventually free mankind in this Dystopian Romance Ménage series.

Cowboys For Christmas
Cowboys Online 1 ~ Moose Ranch
Jan Springer
A Canadian Contemporary Ménage Romance m/f/m/m Series

Jennifer Jane (JJ) Watson has spent the past ten Christmases in a maximum-security prison.

The last thing she expects is to get early parole, along with a job on a remote Canadian cattle ranch serving Christmas holiday dinners to three of the sexiest cowboys she's ever met!

Rafe, Brady and Dan thought they were getting a couple of male ex-cons to help out around their secluded ranch, but instead they get an attractive and very appealing female.

In the snowbound wilds of Northern Ontario, female companionship is rare.

It's a good thing the three men like to share...

They're dominating, sexy-as-sin and they fill JJ with the hottest ménage fantasies she's ever had. Suddenly she's craving cowboys for Christmas and wishing for something she knows she can never have...a happily ever after.

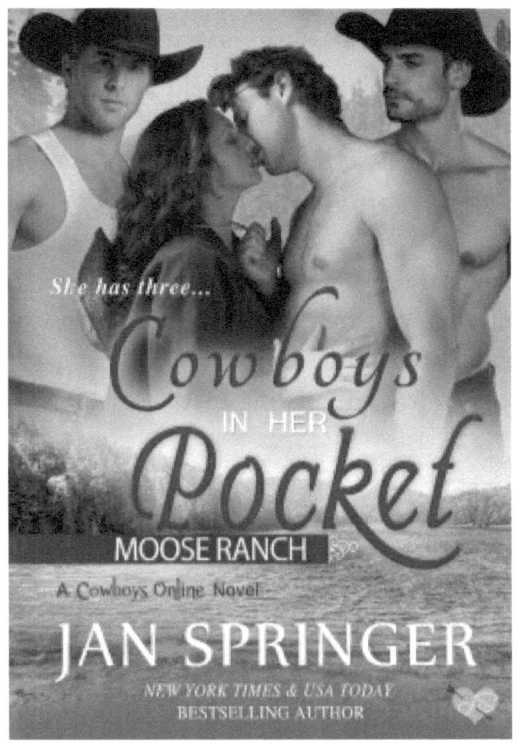

Cowboys In Her Pocket
Cowboys Online 2 ~ Moose Ranch
Jan Springer

After spending ten years in a maximum-security prison Jennifer Jane (JJ) Watson got early parole and a job on a remote Canadian cattle ranch playing housekeeper to three of the sexiest cowboys she's ever met...

Spring has finally arrived at Moose Ranch, and a single woman fresh out of prison shouldn't be experiencing scorching ménages with her three sexy-as-sin cowboys. But JJ's love for her men continues to grow as she gives into the fevered heat and scorching passions she feels for each of them.

Life is perfect.

Until her new life is tested when mysterious happenings occur on the ranch and then one of her cowboys is viciously attacked and injured.

Will JJ's newfound freedom and happiness be ripped away?

Rafe, Brady and Dan never expected to find an attractive and very appealing female to help them out at their secluded ranch. But in the wilds of Northern Ontario, female companionship is rare. It's a good thing the three men like to share...

Brady, Dan and Rafe have never been happier. Their cattle ranch is flourishing and their continued desire to share the sexy woman who cares for them makes their life complete. Until danger threatens to rip everything apart...

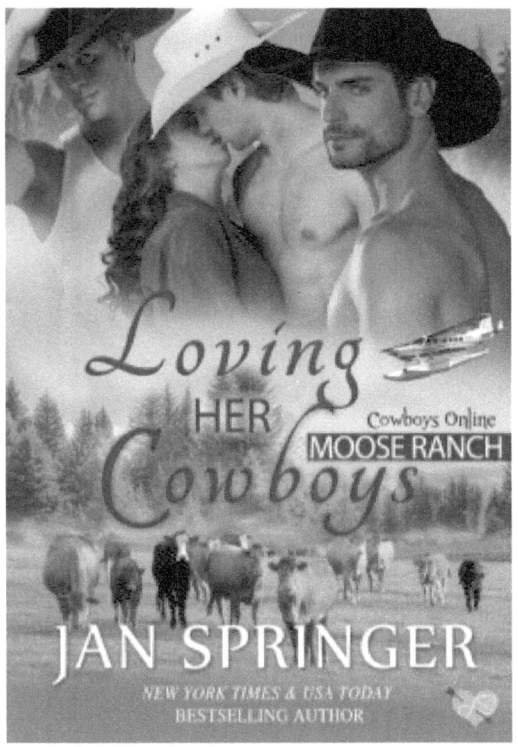

Loving Her Cowboys
Cowboys Online 3 ~ Moose Ranch
Jan Springer

After spending ten years in a maximum-security prison Jennifer Jane (JJ) Watson got early parole and a job on a remote Canadian cattle ranch playing housekeeper to three of the sexiest cowboys she's ever met...

Her love for her cowboys continues to grow as she gives into fevered heat. But JJ's simmering restlessness explodes and she's seriously making up for lost time by pursuing her dreams. There's only one little problem. She hasn't revealed to her bosses what she's been up to while they're away tending to the cattle. She knows when they discover her secret, there will be hell to pay.

Ranchers Rafe, Dan and Brady have found the woman who completes them. She makes their secluded ranch a home-sweet-home. She's vulnerable, sweet and willing to share her bed with all three of them. But when JJ's secret is unwittingly revealed, they're stunned and angry. They figure it's time to dole out some fiery punishment in some mighty naughty ways...

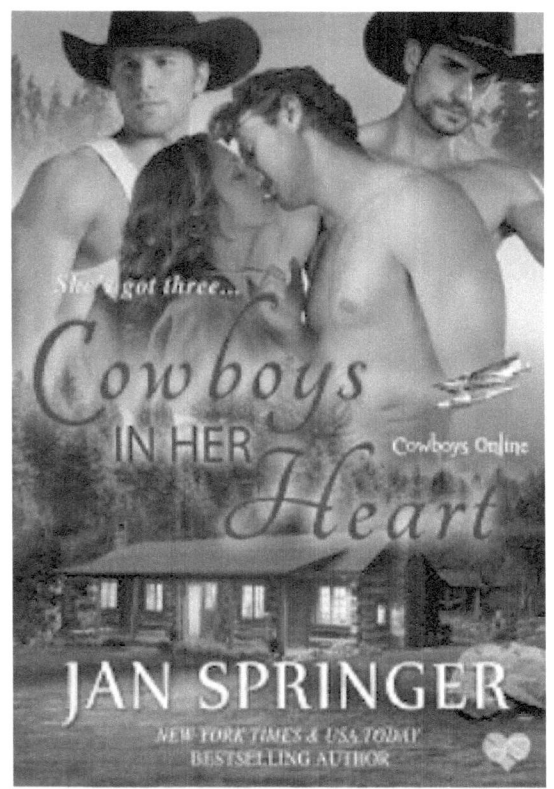

Cowboys In Her Heart
Cowboys Online #4 ~ Moose Ranch
After spending ten years in a maximum-security prison, JJ gets
unexpected parole and a job on a Canadian ranch serving up scrumptious
dinners and lots of hot love to three of the sexiest cowboys she's ever met.
Jennifer Jane "JJ" Watson has never been happier. She's going to have a
baby!

Thankfully their wilderness ranch is a nice distraction for her three sexy cowboys while she's away flying her plane. But when she's home, her dominant hunks are tending to her naughty pregnant cravings and that includes plenty of sizzling ménages.

Rafe, Brady and Dan don't much like the idea of their woman flying the Canadian skies and being at the mercy of the unpredictable Northern Ontario weather. They would prefer having her warming their beds twenty-four seven. But she has a way of getting what she wants and right now she needs her new-found freedom.

Worst fears are realized when JJ, her friend and JJ's plane suddenly go missing and she doesn't come back home to them.

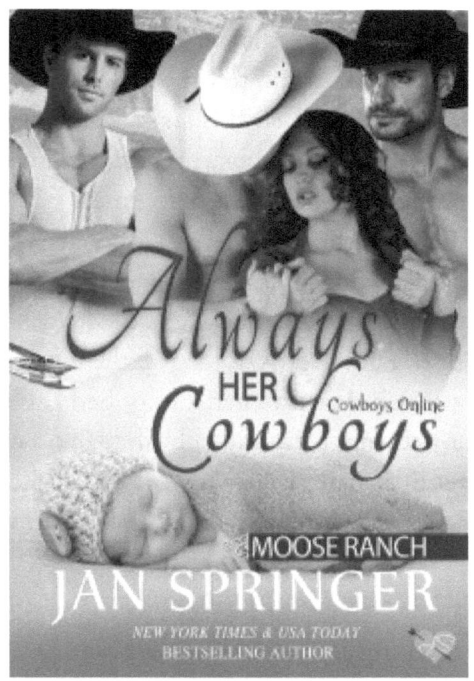

Always Her Cowboys
Cowboys Online 5 ~ Moose Ranch
~Jennifer Jane (JJ) Watson has spent ten Christmases in a
maximum-security prison. The last thing she expects is to get early
parole, along with a job on a remote Canadian cattle ranch serving
Christmas holiday dinners to three of the sexiest cowboys she's ever
met!
Rafe, Brady and Dan thought they were getting male ex-cons to help
out around their secluded ranch, but instead they get an attractive and
very appealing female. In the snowbound wilds of Northern Ontario,

female companionship is rare. It's a good thing the three men like to share...

Christmas is coming once again to Moose Ranch and with the due date of JJ's baby approaching fast, JJ is distracting herself from anxiety attacks by keeping herself ultra-busy preparing for the arrival of her baby and planning Moose Ranch's first annual Christmas party!

In having a wee baby on the way, there's a lot of stress for Brady, Rafe and Dan. Especially due to JJ's decision on having a wilderness mid-wife deliver the baby at the ranch house - with all of them present for the birth! But their concerns don't stop the men from showing JJ how much they love her...out of bed and in!

With wicked snowstorms, a grounded bush plane, a cheerful holiday party and a sweet little baby, the owners of Moose Ranch know this will be one sparkling Christmas season they won't soon forget...

Futuristic Erotic Romance (m/f)

Pleasure Bound ~ The Complete Set ~ Books 1-6

A Hero's Welcome – Book One – Dr. Annie welcomes injured astronaut Joe Hero into her bed every chance she gets.

A Hero Escapes – Book Two – Queen Jacey's forbidden fantasies become reality and she can't get enough of well-hung Ben Hero's sizzling lovemaking.

A Hero Betrayed – Book Three – Fugitive-on-the-run Virgin must save Buck Hero who has been infected by a deadly virus. The cure? A twenty-four-hour making love marathon! But then she must betray him...

A Hero's Kiss – Book Four – US Astronaut Piper Hero is rescued by a dangerous stranger and can't . Why can't seem to keep her hands off his luscious whip-scarred body.

A Hero Wanted – Book Five – A Hero is wanted for plus-sized Jenna who is finally able to explore her intimate side...where menages are welcome.

Captive Heroes – Book Six – While searching for her brothers, Kayla Hero is bound and imprisoned by the Breeders— along with a male captive whose tantalizing scars pique her interest.
Injured and lost in a dense jungle, Kinley Hero is intimidated by the scarred man who hunts her, especially due to the power of erotic submission he holds over her.

Naughty Girl Desires Boxed Set
Contemporary Erotic Romance (m/f)
Includes: Jade's Fantasy, The Biker & The Bride,
Sinderella Sexy and Nice Girl Naughty.

Jade's Fantasy
In the land of the rich and famous, Kidnap Fantasies is the answer to discreet naughty downtime.
When ex-downhill skier Jade Hart's two sisters give her a Kidnap Fantasies questionnaire, Jade is aroused at the prospect of having no-strings fun in the sun with a stranger whose only job would be to fulfill her every intimate fantasy. Although she knows she's too shy to send it in, she secretly pours her deepest wishes into the questionnaire. Soon the questionnaire mysteriously vanishes and Jade's fantasy man appears on her luxury yacht in the form of a sexy handy man who gives her an intimate toy-filled Christmas holiday she'll never forget.

The Biker & The Bride
Wrapped in red-hot lust for revenge, Avery plots to murder the man responsible for the death of her son.
Her plans are dashed when her ex-husband crashes her wedding and whisks her away on his motorcycle to the rustic Canadian wilderness cabin they'd once honeymooned.
Police detective, Mason is fighting for Avery's love with everything he has.
Armed with whipped cream, handcuffs and his undying devotion, Mason vows he will make Avery love again.

But it's only a matter of time before the man she'd planned to kill hunts them down...

Sinderella Sexy

By night, Dr. Ella Cinder, escapes reality by secretly performing in her own naughty version of Cinderella, aptly re-titled Sinderella.

When sexy colleague Dr. Roarke Stephenson appears in the Sinderella audience on the same night her Prince Charming stands her up, Ella Cinder seizes the opportunity to make the man she's secretly fantasized about into her very own Prince Charming for one night of carnal fun in front of an audience.

But at the stroke of midnight, Ella knows she must face the harsh reality that Roarke can never learn her true identity.

Dr. Roarke Stephenson is immediately captured by the mysterious actress who hides her face behind a mask and is known only as Sinderella. For some insane reason, she reminds him of his klutzy co-worker, Ella. But that's not possible. Plain Ella would never have the nerve to do the wickedly delicious things Sinderella does to him, or would she?

Nice Girl Naughty

Blind since nineteen, Summer has blossomed into a famous wood carver.

When she's almost killed by a serial killer, she's whisked away to a secluded wilderness cabin by the man she once secretly loved.

Summer can't get enough of touching professional bodyguard Nick Cassidy's thick, powerful muscles and all those other hard, yummy male body parts that she has always longed to explore.

For years Nick has stayed away from his best friend's kid sister, nice girl Summer. Now he's back, and sweeping his gorgeous redhead into the naughty cravings he's always had for her. With passion blinding him, Nick doesn't realize their hideout isn't safe—until it's too late.

YOU CAN GET A PEEK at more of Jan Springer's Erotic Romances at:

http://www.janspringer.com[1]

Spunky Girl Publishing Erotica
~Jasmine Black~

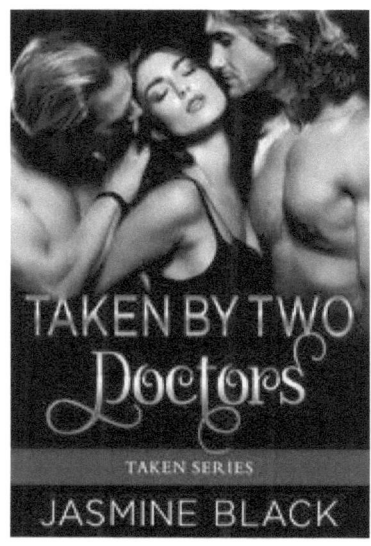

A BDSM Medical Fetish Erotica Quickie MFM

Waitress Jean Spelling, visits her controversial doctor once a month for some much-needed...stress relief. She looks forward to putting her feet up in the stirrups and enjoys Dr. Ball's naughty unconventional treatments. This time when she arrives, she's surprised to discover that she'll be physically examined by two doctors and they'll prescribe her some much-needed release right there on the examination table!

Other eBooks in the Taken series
Taken by Two Firefighters
Taken by Two Bikers
Taken by Two Billionaires
Taken by Two Bosses
Taken by Two Cowboys
Taken by Two Personal Trainers
Taken by Two Carpenters
Taken by Three Bikers
Taken by Three Billionaires

Jasmine Black Website ~ http://www.jasmine-black.com
Twitter ~ @blackerotica1

Ways we can connect:

Jan Springer Website at http://www.janspringer.com[1]
Instagram – http://www.instagram.com/janspringerauthor
Facebook - https://www.facebook.com/janspringereroticromance
Twitter - https://twitter.com/janspringer @janspringer
Pinterest - http://www.pinterest.com/janspringer1/
Jan's Blog - http://janspringerauthor.wordpress.com/blog-2/
LinkedIn - http://ca.linkedin.com/in/janspringerauthor/
Google   Plus   -   https://plus.google.com/u/0/101527334949931513035/posts

Happy Reading,
Jan Springer

---

1. http://www.janspringer.com/

About Jan Springer

Jan Springer writes full-time at her home nestled in cottage country, Ontario, Canada. She enjoys hiking, kayaking, gardening, reading and writing. She is a member of the Romance Writers of America and the Writers Union of Canada.

Here are ways you can connect with Jan Springer:
Jan Springer Website at http://www.janspringer.com[2]
Jan's Newsletter: http://ymlp.com/xguembmugmgb
Instagram – http://www.instagram.com/janspringerauthor
Facebook - https://www.facebook.com/janspringereroticromance
Twitter - https://twitter.com/janspringer @janspringer
Pinterest - http://www.pinterest.com/janspringer1/
Jan's Blog - http://janspringerauthor.wordpress.com/blog-2/
LinkedIn - http://ca.linkedin.com/in/janspringerauthor/

Don't miss out!

Visit the website below and you can sign up to receive emails whenever Jan Springer publishes a new book. There's no charge and no obligation.

https://books2read.com/r/B-A-WGQ-XKIX

BOOKS 2 READ

Connecting independent readers to independent writers.